Love in Spite of Darkness

Ashley S. Henry

ISBN: 1470161443
ISBN-13: 978-1470161446

DEDICATION

Daaiyah 'Day-Day' Washington

ACKNOWLEDGMENTS

I would first like to take the time to acknowledge the fact that I am capable of accomplishing things that I have set out to do. My father in heaven, thank you for blessing me with the gift of literature; it's refreshing to be able to express myself through my writing. My parents, Anita & Ralph; thank you so much for believing, having faith and knowing that my calling is in writing. Thank you for reading every piece of work that I have ever written, even if it was poorly written. My big brothers Chris & Eric and little sister Casche', thanks for telling all your friends how creative your sister is! =) lol getting the word out there how talented I am. Mrs. Barbara Grovner, author of Even Numbers and We Belong Together, for editing my work. I'm thanking you one million times for helping me and giving me advice on the publishing business. Monique Crawford for helping me design the cover, my little cousin Niveka for being on the cover!! Also, I can't forget the following people: Melvin, Zonnika, Jodi, Jean, Rayneek, JaMont, Damesha, Tatjuana, Aunt Ellen, Aunt Pumpkin, Aunt Niecy, Tabitha, and Qiana. Thank you all for ALL of your support, for encouraging me to go after my goal, for believing in me, for reading my work and giving your honest opinion on them! From the bottom of my heart and every vein that runs through it I want to thank all of you for being the hands to push me forward.

Love ya'll!

Chapter 1

If I tell ya'll about the struggle I had to go through to get where I am today, some of you may think I'm a white oleander, beautiful yet dangerous. Others may say I'm the rose Tupac Shakur was talking about when he said: "Did you hear about the rose that grew from a crack in the concrete, proving nature's law wrong it learned to walk without having any feet." In reality I'm just me Nevaeh Smith, the girl who learned not to be scared to let someone love her and found love in a good man; the girl who had her innocence taken by a junkie, and whose mom neglected her to take her medicine. Ya'll may be sitting back saying, "That girl ain't really go through all of that," or "She just tryna get some attention," but see that's where you would be wrong. I have been through it all. I was what you would call an around the way girl. I was like the neighborhood's jump rope: everyone took their turn. Sex, lies, money, betrayal, and death are what would be seeing in my life. Let me take you on a journey through, my life.

I remember it as if it was yesterday. I came home early from school because I was not feeling too well. At the time I was in the fourth grade and I was going to an elementary school a couple of blocks away from my house. I remember one day when I was sick I attempted to call home from school to let my mama know that I wasn't feeling too good and wanted to come home, only to hear a recording letting me know that we no longer had a house phone. After the failed attempt of calling my mama I snuck out of school and walked two blocks to the apartments that we lived in.

I walked into the run-down apartment building clutching my stomach, as I made my way around the soda bottles and the empty beer cans. The building looked as if a tornado had just passed by. The smell of piss cursed the halls. Empty bags of potato chips and weed bags covered the floor. The windows that once brought light into the building were broken out. On my way up the last flight of steps I grabbed the rusty hand rail, which was on the verge of falling, lend over and vomited right where I was standing. Ms. Harrison, my neighbor, was walking out of her apartment when she saw me kneeling in the mess crying. Walking over to me and helping me up she said,

"Nevaeh, what are you doing out of school this early?"

I sniffed before I said, "I don't feel good." I continued to cry. "I want my mommy." My nose was running and my eyes were burning from crying.

"Your mommy's not here. Come in here so I can clean you up." She helped me up and escorted me into her nicely furnished apartment.

When I walk into her apartment the smell of baked apple pie greeted me at the door. I had to take off my shoes before I walked into her home so that I wouldn't get her cream colored carpet dirty. In the living room a cream love seat and a glass table sitting in the front of it would great you. Mirrors and white plastic flowers decorated the white wall above the love seat, and then on the table there were pictures of Ms. Harrison, and then her and my mom when they were in their teenage years, and then her and me.

Looking back at her apartment and the way she lived I wondered why she choose not to live in Bowie, Maryland; where the kids never came outside and the neighborhoods were clean and quiet. Why did she pick Central Gardens to live in, a place where crime was constant. Alcoholics and crack addicts walking around begging people for some change so they can get another hit or swig. People rudely pissing in the hallways, teenagers freely fornicating in the laundry room in the night; little kids outside playing freaky Friday or 'house' not knowing that they're setting themselves up to become parents at a young age. Central Gardens wasn't the type of place to try and raise a child; but still women tried.

Then there were times I wondered why she never married or had kids of her own. I remember when she told me I was like her child so that was one of the reasons why she chose not to have any; but I still wondered why she never married. She was young, in her mid-twenties and she was beautiful. She had golden skin with long thick sandy brown hair. Then there were her eyes; her eyes were beautiful, one day they would be hazel then the next gray. She had nice round hips and her butt was huge. She never wore make up or lipstick; she told me that it hides your natural beauty.

When we walked through the living room we past the dining room and kitchen, she helped me into the dolphin-decorated bathroom, put me in the tub, and helped wash me up. She gave me a large WPGC 95.5 t-shirt that came to my feet, fed me some chicken noodle soup and gave me some ginger ale. Then she sent me off to get some rest in her queen size bed.

I was sleep for about three hours, but it only seemed like five minutes. I woke up to the sound of the vacuum outside of Ms. Harrison's bedroom door and a bad cramp in my stomach. I climbed off of the bed and looked down at the t-shirt I had on. There was blood on it. When I looked on the bed there was blood on there as well. I didn't know what to do so I ran to Ms. Harrison. When I told her what was going on and where the blood was coming from she put me back in the tub then told me what was happening. She told me that I had just started my period; she told me everything that I needed to know about it. Some of the stuff she was telling me my older sister Heaven told me right before they took her away. Ms. Harrison and I stayed up half the night talking. There wasn't much that we could talk about because I was only nine, but she did tell me that I started young and that it was rare but not unusual. She also told me that my body is changing. There would be days I would feel like being bothered and days I wouldn't. She also told me that I could get pregnant now if I had sex with a boy and it only takes one time.

I woke up around two o'clock the next day to the sound of Ms. Harrison and my mom going back and forth at it. I got up and stood in the hallway.

"So are you gonna let Nevaeh stay with me for awhile, until you get yourself together?" Ms. Harrison asked my mom.

"No, she's not staying with you." My mom retorted.

"She started her cycle last night,"

"Already, she's only nine,"

"They start early,"

"Just go get her so I can talk to her." My mom fanned Ms. Harrison off.

"I already talked to her last night,"

"Oh, so now you wanna be her mother?" my mom asked her with attitude.

"I've always been there for her!" Ms. Harrison said in anger. I have never seen her so mad before. I have seen her and my mom get into arguments over me before, but she had never gotten that mad.

"Nicole go and get the damn child!" My mom demanded. She was drunk. I could tell by her posture and her mood and by the way her words slurred. It was times like this when I wished Ms. Harrison were really my mother. Ms. Harrison began to talk through her teeth, "If you want her, go and get her your damn self." She stood her ground and folded her arms over her small breast; my mom starred Ms. Harrison in the eyes as she called out for me.

"Nevaeh get in here, we're leaving." I jumped to the sound of her voice then quickly moved into their eyesight. I stood before them with my head down and hands behind my back as if I had done something wrong and was about to get into trouble. My mom yanked me by the arm pulling me towards the door, and then I felt myself being pulled the other way. We stopped and looked at Ms. Harrison.

"LaWanda you're thirty-four years old, you have this child living with you, it's time for you to get your shit together." Ms. Harrison said.

"I'm a grown ass woman. Don't tell me what to do or how to raise *my* child." With that said she marched out of the apartment, dragging me along.

Living with my mama was not a happy home, but it also wasn't hell. Our home was nothing like Ms. Harrison's. We did not have wall to wall cream colored carpet; instead we had American Cherry wood floors. Instead of the smell of baked apple pie greeting me when I first walk into our home, I get knocked over by the strong aroma of marijuana. A couple of art pieces decorated the wall along with baby pictures of me and my sister Heaven. Roaches began to find a home in our kitchen; dishes began to pile up on top of the counter. There was never food in the house but I never had anything to worry about because I knew that whenever I got hungry that Ms. Harrison would feed me.

I remember when I turned ten my mom had met a man name Rodney. I knew from the moment that I seen him that he was no good for my mom. He introduced her to the drugs that she abused. At first she was an alcoholic. Beer was the first thing she ran to in the morning to wake her up. Then it escalated to crack; heroin; PCP; love boat, everything else you could name. Rodney was black as oil; around his late thirties, baldhead and chunky; chunky like Gerald Lavert. I was sitting in my Barbie decorated room one Saturday afternoon playing with my dolls while my mom was in the room sleep and Rodney was watching our 24' color television in the living room. Or so I thought, until he came in my room and sat on my twin size bed, sinking it in from the large amount of body weight he carried. He started watching me. He was there for a good five minutes when he told me to come here so he could give me something. I went and sat on his lap like I always did, waiting for the gift. He always gave me some kind of toy; most of the dolls in my room came from him. That's one thing I did like about him though, he gave me all the toys a little girl could ever want; but I never thought the gift that I was about to receive would corrupt me for the rest of my life.

He started to feel all over me; I began to feel very uncomfortable, I tried to get up but he wouldn't let me. He put his hand up my pink skirt and pushed my heart panties to the side and started rubbing on what I called my special area. I wanted to get up and run over to Ms. Harrison's house but he wouldn't let me. I tried to cry out for my mama but nothing would come out. He put his hands all over my undeveloped body, before he lay me down on my bed. I kicked and screamed and cried; no one had ever put his or her hands on me the way that he did. He held me down with one hand and pulled my panties down with the other one. I squeezed my legs together, as I tried to wiggle free from his grasp. Silent tears fell from my eyes. I saw his pants drop to his ankles. Somehow he estranged my legs apart and the next thing I knew I was crying out for someone to come and save me. That was not the way I fantasized about losing my virginity. I wasn't in my twenties. There was no white dress, I didn't have a husband and we for damn sure weren't in the Bahamas. Instead we were in my Barbie decorated room, no wedding dress, no husband, just a chunky black man with liquor seeping through his pores. I was just a baby. After he finished he left me in my room stricken; I hurt so badly that I cried, I cried myself to sleep that afternoon.

When I woke up my tiny body was so sore. It was so hard for me to move out of the spot where I had cried myself to sleep. Bruises hid on the inside of my thighs, I couldn't close my legs once I had gotten out of my bed. I went into the hallway and looked towards my mom's door. It was cracked and a light was coming out. I went into her room to tell her about the horrible event that happened earlier. When I opened the door I saw Rodney putting his face into the chipped, cherry oak colored nightstand and sniffing up a white substance. My mom was on the other side of the room sticking a needle into her arm. I saw her doing the same thing last week, but she told me it was her medicine. I knew better than to believe that. I was young but I wasn't stupid.

"Mommy I have to tell you something," I said.

"Okay I'll be out there in just a minute. Let mommy finish what she's doing." My mom said to me.

"But it's very important," I whined.

"You see me trying to do something, get outta here, go some got-damn where, and I'll talk to you when I finish." She ordered me. I looked at her then glanced at Rodney, he had his head bent back rubbing his face. I shook my head at the two inconsiderate people that lingered in the room, and I left and went back into my room. I never told my mom about what happened to me. Even though she never admitted it, I knew she already knew how that man invaded my body; she just chose not to believe it.

Chapter 2

Lawanda White that was my moms' name; she was beautiful or at least used to be. She had the best shape with the measurements 36, 24, 36. Every man wanted her, but one man caught her eye. He was mixed with Hispanic and black and he had jet-black hair, straight white teeth and dimples. His name was Jonathon Smith. He and mom got together when they were in high school together for two years before they had my sister Heaven' four years later, they had me. Nevaeh Maria Smith.

My third birthday is one that I would never forget. I don't have any memories of my dad except for the day of May 25, 1981. My mom, dad, Heaven, and I were on our way to the park to have a little family cookout for my birthday. We decided to walk because it was such a nice day outside and it was just down the street. My dad had me on his back and we were all talking about what we were going to do at the park when these men called my dad over to this black Mercedes. I recognized the guy that was sitting in the car; it was one of my dads' best friends, uncle John. At first they were talking casually, and then one of the men inside the car started yelling. Next I saw my dad backing up from the car with his hands up as uncle John extended his arm out the window then:

Boom! Boom!

It looked like fire came from out of Uncle John's hands. I watched as he fell to the ground. Everything was moving in slow motion. Everyone was running, and cars were speeding off. My mom dragged us by my father's side. She fell down beside him and cried. Lifeless on the ground my dad lay. I didn't know what to do, so I just stood there and looked; no type of emotions was shown. I'm not sure of why Uncle John killed daddy. They were supposed to be brothers. Uncle John came to daddy's funeral and tried to act sentimental, he even started to cry. Those were the last tears that he cried, because a week or two after the funeral my mom sent my daddy brothers to handle him. It came on the news weeks later. They sent him swimming with the fish.

After that terrible tragedy is when my mom started drinking more than she usually did, and began doing things she normally didn't do. She started taking all her anger and frustration out on Heaven, just because she was the oldest, and Heaven would just tell me,

"She just jealous of my body, because I get more attention from her male friends than she does." Heaven pranced around the house in her little shorts, especially when mama had her male friends over. When mama wasn't looking she would give little eye contact to them, sometimes she would give them a little peep show, depending on what she had on that day. If I would've done something wrong she would get on Heaven; she would say,

"You should have been looking after her. You're the oldest." All that time I thought I was her child not Heaven's. Why did Heaven have to take care of me when she was just a child herself? Mama would have sex with all these different men. Young, old, it didn't matter the age just as long as she got whatever she requested in the end. I walked in on mama giving a male or female pleasure with the same lips she would kiss me in the morning with. Whenever mama would do something men didn't like they would beat on her. Some even beat her so bad they put her in the hospital. She was longing so much for the attention that she use to receive from my dad that she didn't care that she became someone's footstool. That was one thing I promised myself; I wouldn't care if a man ever cursed me out or called me out of my name. I don't even care if I loved him, but I wouldn't become any mans footstool. I wouldn't allow him to walk all over me.

I remember a time when I was six. I had just come home from Ms. Harrison's house playing with her niece Robin. When I walked into the room Heaven and I shared my heart stopped; one of my mom's boyfriends was mounting on top of Heaven, hurting her. Tears were pouring out of her eyes. I didn't know what to do. She looked at me and I could see the pain she felt, a pain I never seen in her before. I couldn't stand to sit there and look at what he was doing to her. "Get off my sister," I yelled as I ran up to them and jumped on his back. He struggled to stay on top of her when I poked him in the eye. He threw me on the floor and pulled himself out of her. He pulled his clothes up and left. I went and lay beside her as she cried. When it first happened I thought she deserved what she got, I mean she was always prancing around the house in these men face; but then I came to realization that no one deserves to get raped no matter what you do.

The next day she tried to tell my mom what happened but my mom dismissed her (she was good at doing that to us) because she was busy on the phone with the man who violated Heaven. The next thing I knew Heaven ran away. I was eight years old and left to deal with all the pain and confusion.

*

I came home from school a cold November day ready to get some rest because we were on Thanksgiving break. I walked into the house to hear Rapper's Delight blasting from the speakers that were in the dining room. I saw my mom in the living room with a bunch of men surrounding her. She looked over their shoulders and saw me standing there watching. This one man with razor bumps and pimples on his face turned and looked at me then back at my mom. Moments later she took me into the back room closed the door.

"You love me right?" my mom asked me. She knew I loved her and I would do anything for her. I knew right where this was headed because she did this once before. I nodded my head yes. "Okay, well them guys want to just touch you, they're not gonna hurt you. I promise." She said that the last time, but they did do something. Right when my self-esteem was rising, they knocked it right back down.

"Okay," I said. My mom took me back into the living room and let those men do whatever they wanted to do to me. I just laid there and let them do their business praying that it would soon end. I was past the physical hurt, but I was now getting hurt mentally and emotionally. I was distraught over that whole ordeal. I couldn't believe my mama would go that low to get another hit. Never in a million years. I turned my head from the men and looked at my mama while she sat on the side taking her 'medicine'. She turned into another crack head sitting outside the apartment building waiting for someone to come outside so she could bum-rush him r her. At that point is when I simply lost all the respect I had for my mom. To me she was just like another woman on the street I didn't know. I wanted to run over to Ms. Harrison like I always did, but I couldn't anymore. She moved away about three months before. So that night I waited until my mama was sound asleep then went and packed some clothes and I ran, I ran as far as my little legs could take me, away from all the stress and all the pain, an eleven year old girl away from home.

*

"Excuse me sir, do you have any change?" I asked a well dressed black man for some money so that I could eat. For almost a year I lived on the streets. Sleeping in abandoned buildings, on the ground, on heaters, at the bus station, on the train, everywhere a little girl my age wasn't suppose to be. In the daytime I sat at Gallery Place metro station and began begging. At first I was ashamed, but when the hunger pains started to kick in I had no choice but to start begging. I continued to go to school for awhile just for lunch, but when the kids started to recognize how dirty I had gotten I just stopped going.

The man looked at me as if he had smelt something of such bad odor, I knew I didn't stink because I had just gone into the bathroom of the Popeye's restaurant and did my daily wash up. I learned early that no matter where I go to make sure I'm clean down there; because I wouldn't want to be picked up funky. I smiled up at the man not wanting to ruin my chances of getting a decent meal for the day. I watched as he dug into the pocket of his navy blue suit and retrieved his wallet. I anxiously waited for the money that I was about to receive. By the way he dressed I was sure that I was about to receive a crisp five dollar bill, but instead he handed me a wrinkled up dollar and fifty cents. I smiled up at the man, but disappointment was written all over my face.

"Thank you sir," I thanked him, not wanting to sound selfish. When the man turned around to walk away I frowned up my face, at least he could've given me fifty more cents so that I could buy chips *and* a soda. I realized that I wasn't getting any money that day at that station so I decided to walk to Foggy Bottom Metro Station. There is where I met my newfound friend Janette Floyd; she to be homeless and living on the streets. I picked up my black book bag, which at one point in time was red, and put it on my back. We walked until we reached the subway over on W street by George Washington Hospital. We walked in Subway restaurant and sat down and got to know each other a lot better. I looked around and watched all of the nice people dressed up in there best Sunday attire come in and out of the store on this nice but cold Sunday afternoon.

"I'm so glad I found someone who was around my age. I didn't want to be alone anymore." I paused, taking a look at the old couple walking into the store hand in hand. "Where is your family?" I finally asked her after a couple minutes of silence.

"I don't know. I never met them before." She started. "All I know is my mother gave me up when I was born. I was adopted into a nice family, but I felt so uncomfortable with them. So I ran away. Living out in these streets is no joke, and I want to go back, but I'm scared that they're not going to want me anymore."

"I would die if I never had the chance to spend time with my mother," every night I would cry for my mama, wishing that I would come looking for me; but she never did.

"Yeah, well you'll get over it." She sighed. "Where is your family?" she asked. I was hoping she was not going to ask me that. If I spoke of it then all of my past hurt and pain would resurface.

"It's a long story," I told her.

"I mean, we have time. Where else do we have to go?" She reminded me. She was right; we did have all the time in the world; nowhere to be and nothing to do. So I told her. She sat there listened, nodding to everything as if she was subjected to the things that I was. She wasn't, it was safer in the streets than it was in that house.

"A year, one whole year and she haven't come looking for me yet." I tried to fight back the tears that I have been holding in since the day that I left home. I took a deep breath. "How old are you?" I asked her.

"Thirteen, I just turned thirteen two months ago, August 29." She informed me. "How old are you?" she asked me.

"Well, I'm eleven. My birthday is on May 25." She shook her head as if to say okay. "So what do you like to do for fun?"

"Read, there is this really good library that I like going to in Maryland. I don't know the name of it but I know it is off of Addison Road, in Fairmont Heights." She told me as her eyes lit up. I scrunched me face. She laughed a little. "I'll just take you over there," she stood up about to leave when she looked at me still sitting down. "Come on."

Chapter 3

Since the day at Subway Janette and I were always together. Over the months she became my only family. At times when we would be sitting in the stair way of hotels we would reminisce about what we been through, and we would talk about our features. Janette often thought about going back to the family that had adopted her. I really didn't want her to go there because then she would be leaving me by myself out in the streets.

"I want to go back to my adopted parents," she would tell me.

"Why? Stay with me, and one day we can get a good job and even get an apartment together," I begged of her.

"Ne-Ne, why don't you just go to one of those group homes? I heard that they were nice, and you don't have to worry about being switched from home to home because you're already at a stable place until you turn eighteen. Plus they will put you back in school." she tried to pursue me. I sighed then rolled my eyes.

One cold December night while we were roaming the streets of uptown Washington DC a 92' dark blue Grand Marquees pulled up beside us. I looked over at the car.

"Just keep walking Ne-Ne," I heard Janette say, but I wasn't paying her too much attention. My main focus was on the car that drove beside us. The tinted windows rolled down.

"Wassup cutie?" This dark skin man with dreads spoke. Janette continued to walk as I stopped and began to talk to the man in the car.

"Nothin, tryna find somewhere to go," I stated. I knew he could tell by the dirty clothes that I had on that I was homeless; but I don't think he cared too much. "Wassup with you tonight?"

"Not a damn thing. So you say you looking for somewhere to go," I shook my head answering him. "Why don't you come and stay at my crib, you and your friend." he told me. I was a little uneasy about going with this guy when I didn't even know him, but I was also tired and ready to go into a warm environment. I looked back at Janette; she had stopped walking and was now starring at me.

"What's your name?" I asked him.

"Bryon, what's yours?"

"Nikki," I told him giving him a false name. "That's Jasmine over there," he nodded his head, then reached out and began to rub my thigh. I became tense at his touch, but I didn't want to stop him and have him thinking that I was immature so I let him feel up on me.

"So I'm saying, ya'll gonna come or what?" he asked me in a low but sexy tone. It didn't take me long to make my decision. The difficult part was getting Janette to go with me. After minutes of convincing Janette to come with me, she reluctantly agreed and got into the car.

When we walked into his apartment I observed my surroundings. It was small on the inside, one bed room. The things that were in his apartment looked brand new, everything, from the glass coffee table to the plasma TV that entertained the living room. A tall Bryon walked over to the kitchen that connected to the living room and went into his top cabinet and pulled out a bottle then turned back to us.

"Ya'll drink?" he asked. Janette shook her head. I on the other hand wanted to seem more mature. I shook my head yes. "Bet!" he said nodding his head as he turned back around and made us some drinks. Janette yanked my arm making me face her.

"Nevaeh, what the hell. NO! You are not about to drink with this man." she told me with a stern look.

"Janette, we need some place to stay tonight. It's too cold outside;

it's just going to be one drink." I tried to reason with her.

"We've been out in worst," she told me.

"Just chill out, and enjoy the night in a warmer environment," Bryon told her as he came up behind me and handed me my cup. I grabbed the cup then gave her pleading eyes; once she rolled her eyes I put a grin on my face then turned to Byron.

"What do you have me drinking?"

"Vodka and Cranberry juice," he told me before taking a sip of his own.

One hour and three drinks later I was loose. Bryon had moved me to his bedroom, the voice of Sada blared through the speakers. My head hung low as I sung the words to 'smooth operator'. I was in the zone when I felt two warm hands rub on my arms up and down and wet lips touch my neck. I shivered at his touch. I leaned forward hopping that he would stop touching me.

"Come on girl, I'm givin you a place to stay for the night, the least you could do is give me some." he told me. I shook my head. "Shit, well then get the fuck out." he told me. I looked at him. My head started to wonder to Janette sleeping peacefully on the couch, underneath warm blankets; then my mother voice popped back into my head telling me the message she had told me once before about using what I have.
I stood up in front of him.
He looked. Nervously I took my shirt off and threw it on the other side of the room. Pushed him back on the bed and climbed on top of him.

I woke up early the next morning before the sun had even risen. I turned over and seen Bryon sleeping on side of me with the sheets only covering the lower area. I sat up and I felt myself developing a headache. I closed my eyes and began to shake my head from side to side. When I opened my eyes I looked back at him to make sure he was still sleep. I slid out of his bed making sure not to wake him, and found my clothes in a pile by the bed, after putting them on I crept over to his dresser and opened the top drawer sliding out a box. I watched him place money in there when we entered his room the night before. I sat it on top of the dresser and stuffed all the money that I can fit into my pocket and placed the box back into the drawer. I crept out of the room and into the living room where Janette slept; I woke her up while in the process of handing her, her worn out payless shoes.

"What are you doing?" Janette whined, as she tried to wiggle her feet from out of my possession. I finally got both of her shoes on. I stood up and pulled her up with me.

"I can't explain right now, but we can't stay here." I informed her. I put her arm around my shoulder and escorted her to the door. I undid his top lock; it made a loud clicking noise. I looked back at his room praying that he wouldn't wake up until we were long gone.

"What did you do? Why are we leaving Nevaeh?" she asked me. I didn't say anything, just shook my head and proceeded to open the door and left, I was scared for the life of both of us, because I did not know what he was going to be capable of when he wake up at sunrise. We ran as far as our tired bodies could take us never to see him again.

We made it to the Renaissance Hotel by the time everyone was up getting ready for their busy work day. We were sitting in the cold stairwell, I was thinking of what to do next with all of this money, but nothing seemed to come to mind. My back was against the wall as Janette lay stretched out on the floor with her head on my lap. It was nothing but silence between the both of us. It was the occasional closing of the doors out in the hallway and the opening and closing of the elevator.

"Nevaeh?" Janette said breaking the silence.

"Yeah,' I said with my eyes closed.

"Did you have sex with him?" My eyes shot open from the question she asked me. I didn't wanna think about what I had done but that was the only thing that I could have thought about to help us out in the situation that we were in.

"What?" I asked as if I was clueless.

"You heard me, did-you-have-sex-with-him?" She asked me,

breaking up the sentence like I was slow. I looked straight ahead at the chipped gray wall.

"I had to do something. We needed somewhere to stay, and he said that he would put us out if I didn't. So, I thought about the situation that we were in and used what I had to get what I wanted. What we needed."

She sighed before saying, "Don't do that again, you don't know what these niggas got out here," she told me. "No, but I know what he had," I told her as a smile crept up on my face.

"What are you talking about?" I dug my hand deep into the pockets of my ashy black jeans and pulled out four rolls of one hundred dollar bills, and dropped them all on the top of her head. She sat up straight as soon as the first roll landed in front of her eye sight. She looked at me shaking her head. I nodded still smiling.

"You thieving bitch," she called me. I laughed as she gave me a light shove. She picked up a roll and then began to go crazy. "Oh my God! Okay, first we gotta go get us a new outfit, then get our hair done, and...Oh no! We need to go to Horn and Horns." I laughed. It was good to put a smile on my best friends face.

*

"Nikki, would you come on!" I heard Janette yell my way. I was talking to this sophisticated white boy just outside of George Washington University. It was now spring, April to be exact. The weather had broken through and with the money that I was making Janette and I had a brand new wardrobe. I had just met the sophisticated white boy an hour ago and we went up to his dorm room. We were chilling in there just talking when his roommate came into the room. They both were well built dudes so I was kind of scared of what might happen but I was not about to let them see the fear that I was trying to hide.

"So what you gonna do?" the first sophisticated dude that I met asked me. Just before his roommate walked into the room he had just given me the decision to either have sex with him or go down on him.

"What's in it for me?" I asked putting on my most sexual voice. With the new clothes that I had brought myself I looked so much older than I was, I was filling out faster than I had noticed. I still didn't have much breast but my ass was bigger than an eighteen year old. If only these men know that they were sexing a minor.

"What are you gonna do?" he asked.

"Well, since the both of you are here, I don't mind giving ya'll a taste." I told him. I glanced at his roommate, his eyes lit up. "But, but there is a fee." They both looked at each other. "A hundred, each; if you don't want to pay it I'll be glad to leave. I do know my way out." I told them as I stood getting ready to leave. The first sophisticated boy that I met stopped me by grabbing my arm and laying me on his bed. The time frame that it took for me to sex both of them only lasted about thirty minutes if not less.

I held up a finger telling Janette that I would be just a minute. When you see Janette and I together you would think that I was the oldest even though I was two years behind her. At times she acted like she was a baby, always wanting to be up under me and never wanting to be alone. When I actually sit and think about it, and it comes to me, she never had someone to be there for her or to take her side. I guess she was looking for guidance and support. But I was not the one to look up to, because I couldn't even take care of myself. After collecting my money from the boys I walked up to Janette and linked arms with her. My tall body over powered her short frame. She gave a blank stare straight ahead.

"How much did you make this time?" she asked me.

"Two hundred," I told her.

"Can we go eat?" she asked me. I nodded my head then lead her to Subway, her favorite place to eat. We went in and I sat down at a table after giving Janette some money to buy her a sandwich, I wasn't hungry. I sat starring out of the window thinking about the way my life could've been if I had another family, people who actually cared about me. Janette came to the table and began eating. It was quiet between the two of us, a little too quiet.

"I'm moving back," she said. I looked at her; she was looking down at her food.

"Moving back where?" I asked already knowing where she was talking about.

"With my adopted parents," I wanted to cry but I refused to. Instead I whined.

"Why? I thought we said that we were gonna be roommates,"

"We still can, when we get older. Nevaeh I can't be living in these streets anymore. I'm ready to go back to school, because I want to be something in life." She said to me. Tears were forming in my eyes. She continued. "I've been talking to my foster mother this last month. She said I can come home, she told me to tell you that there are good group homes out here."

"You said that you was always going to be with me," I was crying by then. "When are you going back?" I asked her.

"Hopefully tonight,"

"Where is the house that you live?"

"I don't know, my mom said that all I have to do is call her and she would come and pick me up."

"Your mom," I laughed to myself. "Your mom left you when you were born. That lady is not your mother!" I screamed to her. I wanted her to stay with me.

"You're just mad that I have someone to take care of me and love me, and care about where I am. Don't get mad, you know that you have a place to go, you just chose not to!" She screamed at me. After a second of us looking at each other she stood up and left.

Chapter 4

It was two months since Janette had moved back with her foster parents. Before her foster mother picked her up from Addison Road Metro Station she gave me her number and told me to call her whenever I feel the need to talk to her. I was so mad at her for leaving me that I didn't call her for a couple months. I was still being my usual self. I was still out sleeping with every man that I came in contact with making sure that I received my money. I remember one night I was walking the streets on Addison Road South looking for somewhere to go for the night, when I sat on the side of the street and began to cry. I was so lonely and confused, I wanted a place to stay and rest my head not having to worry about looking behind my back whenever I went to sleep behind grocery stores or inside of apartment buildings. I reached into the new red book bag that I had just brought and pulled out a sheet of paper that had the number to the place where Janette was staying, along with an address that I had gotten from her after I had talked to her a couple of weeks ago.

I walked to the address that she had given me and looked at the house that I wished I lived in. the perfectly cut grass, the white picket fence, and the porch that brought the house to life. I walked through the fence and walked to the door. I hesitated before I knocked. I knocked three more times before the door opened and I stood face to face with Janette. "Hey Janette," I smiled.

"What are you doing here?" she asked me, more shocked than happy.

"I wanna know if I can stay the night. Just for the night, I will leave in the morning, first thing in the morning." I said to her. More like begged.

"Who's that at the door Nette?" her adopted mother appeared at the door. From the looks of the woman who stood before me you could tell Janette was adopted. Janette's adopted mother stood almost six feet tall, smooth chocolate skin, and thick nappy hair that needed a perm every two weeks. Janette only stood four-foot-eleven, caramel skin and thick silky hair that looked like tracks. Janette looked at the woman.

"I'll be in there in just a minute," she told her adopted mother. The woman looked at me then back at Janette before shaking her head and going back into the house.

"Nevaeh, you can't come here," sadness resurfaced and displayed on my face. I wanted to cry again, just like the time when she told me that she was going to go back home. "I didn't mean that. I mean what's wrong?" I looked at her.

"I just need somewhere to stay for the night. I'll be gone in the morning. I swear." Janette looked at me with sympathy in her eyes.

"I'm sorry Nevaeh, you just can't. I told you where you should go." Tears streamed out of my eyes.

"Can I at least have something to eat or drink?" I asked her. She hesitated before she nodded her head then turned and went in her house. Shutting the door behind her, not even inviting me in. she came out a couple minutes later with food on a paper plate and a can fruit punch soda. I looked at her and took the plate as I said thank you, letting her know I appreciate her help. Then, I left.

A month after I had turned fifteen, which was a year after I had gone to see Janette. I was being released from the hospital after a brutal beating I had received from a group of girls; one of the females accused me of sleeping with her man. I was not sure if I did sleep with her man because I was sexing about five men a day. When I meet them the first thing they say to me was not "My name is Mike and I have a girlfriend. Are you ready to fuck now?" So all the men that I was having sex with were single as far as I knew.

After I was released from the hospital I had to follow a social worker, Ms. Cummings. She was the first person who I seen when I woke up after my minor surgery. I found Ms. Cummings very beautiful; the dark skin that she possessed reminded me of the tar construction workers pour on the road. She had long thin legs made for walking down the runway for Versace. The tracks that she wore shaped her oval face bringing her almond shape eyes to life. She questioned me about my parents. I told her that I did not know who my parents where. Then she asked me how long I lived in the streets. I told her all my life.

While we were in Ms. Cummings '93' royal blue Toyota Caroler, silence fell between us. Ms. Cummings was staring straight ahead at the road, while I was staring out the window. I watched as we left from DC and headed into Maryland, until we pulled up to a big house that sat on the corner of Southern Ave. She turned the car off and got out; she walked in front of the car and waited until I got out. It took her awhile before she noticed that I was not going anywhere. She turned and looked at me giving me this stern look telling me to get out of the car now. I got out of the car, Ms. Cummings started to walk up to the front door, and I followed. She knocked on the door a couple of times before someone answered. My stomach was doing summersaults. This tall dark chocolate, baldhead, with bedroom eyes appeared in front of the door. His well defined body showed through his muscle tight shirt. He had sexy brown lips that matched his body. The man grabbed his suit case that was sitting beside the door.

"Hey, how you doing, she's inside. Tracie, the social worker is here." with that said he hurried out of the door. Ms. Cummings and I walked into the house and into the living room to be greeted by a forty-four year old woman. The lady had rich caramel skin, long sunset red dreads, with an annoying high pitch voice. As we stood in the living room and observed my surroundings as the two women talked. The living room was black and gold at the time. black carpet; black leather seats with black and gold pillows; black coffee table with gold trims; big screen T.V. and a painting of a man sitting on the steps with his head lowered, a black hat on his head; and a saxophone in his hand like he's playing it. Gold ornaments danced upon the wall.

"Sharita!" Ms. Adams yelled in an annoying high pitched voice. She flung her dreads out of her face. Her caramel skin reminded me of a payday bar. I continued to observe the place where I was going to be resting my head until I turned eighteen. I watched as a short chubby girl walked into the room.

"Lisa where is Sharita?" I focused my attention on Ms. Adams then looked at my case worker. Ms. Cummings tossed me a sincere smile.

"Last time I seen her she was up stairs on the phone," this stumpy girl said. The girl was only five-foot around the same height as Janette. Her complexion was the same as Ms. Adams; her hair was thick and nappy, she looked sweet, but looks are very deceiving.

"Well go upstairs and tell her I said get off of that phone and come here," she told Lisa. Lisa shook her head then ran up the stairs, a couple seconds later a very thin girl appeared on the stairway.

"Huh?" She asked.

"Come show uh-" Ms. Adams looked at me.

"Nevaeh," I said putting a false smile on my face.

"Come show Nevaeh where she will be sleeping." Ms. Adams said. Sharita motioned her head for me to follow her. I looked at Ms. Cummings for reassurance; she shook her head letting me know that everything was going to be okay. Sharita and I went up stairs to this nice sized room; there was a twin-size bed on each side of the room and a '27'-inch T.V. in the middle of the room. The walls were pale and plain; the bed had plain white sheets on them, and nothing a teen girl would have in her room. It looked like the room was decorated out of a penitentiary home edition magazine.

"Your bed is over there," Sharita said as she pointed to the bed next to the wide window. I watched as she flopped on her bed and picked up the phone. Sharita wasn't big as a minute. She was about five-

five and as skinny as a toothpick. She had penny brown skin, brown long braids in her hair, and light brown contacts in her eyes. There was a phone in every room and there were two phone lines, one for the kids and one for the adults.

After I finished unpacking the two bags of clothes that I had about twenty minutes later Sharita had managed to call her boyfriend Kelvin, I know his name because she kept calling him when they were arguing. They were arguing about him not taking her to the movies like he promised. She cried and whined to him but he still came out with an excuse. I shook my head at her. I was tired of listening to her cry so I walked out the room and into the hallway. I heard music blasting from one of the rooms down the hall. As I got closer to the door the poetic lyrics of Tupac's song *Brenda's Gotta Baby* became more recognizable. When I got up to the door it was slightly opened. I peeked inside. No one was in there from the angle that I was looking at anyway. I pushed the door open just a little more trying to see if I can see more than just a drawing board.

"What you doing?" I heard a deep voice behind me. I jumped and turned around coming face to face with a breath taking appearance. The boy had hypnotizing grey eyes buttermilk skin, low cut fade, and his body frame was fine from what I could see through his clothes.

"Uh, um, No," I stuttered. He smiled. My heart stopped and something had got caught in my throat to where I could not talk. Dimples hid within his face.

"Excuse me, I need to get into my room," I heard him say, but my feet wouldn't move. He laughed. Leaned over and whispered into my ear.

"You keep staring at me like that then I'm gonna take you in the room and turn you inside out." then he took his tongue and licked my ear. The heat from his breath brought me out of my daze. I rolled my eyes letting him know that I was not turned on by his sexual demeanor. I moved to the side letting him enter his room.

"I was just trying to meet the people in the house." I told him. I watched him as he moved leisurely around the room. I stood in his doorway with my hands rested on my large hips.

"So what's your name?" I asked. He didn't say anything; he just moved to me and stood there.

"Quintin," he gave me another one of his breath taking smiles. I put a grin on my face. He slowly backed up then turned around into his room. I followed him and stood beside his bed.

"You don't have a roommate?" I asked. He shook his head no. I began to walk around the room to get a feel of it. The drawings that he had everywhere were fascinating. "How long have you lived here?" I asked another question.

"Since I was a baby," he told me. I nodded my head. I walked up to a drawing that he had sitting on a desk by the small window.

"Where did you learn to draw?"

"My dad," he told me.

"Oh, so you know your parents?" I stopped my snooping and asked.

"Uh, yeah. The Adams is the only parents that I have ever had. They adopted me two months after I was born and took care of me since then. So, yeah I look at them like they're my birth parents."

"Oh okay," I said as I walked over to the bed and sat on it. I began to watch him as he moved from different areas of his room cleaning up. I leaned back on his comfortable queen sized bed rubbing my hand across his royal blue silk sheets. My pinky found a warm place inside of my mouth. I found it quiet soothing to fall asleep with one of my fingers inside of my mouth while rubbing on something soft.

A sharp pain ran through my stomach causing me to awake from my sleep. When my eyes focused I noticed that I wasn't in the bed that I had fallen asleep in. I looked around the room and seen the T.V. on and seen a shadow on the other side of the room.

"Baby I thought you said that you were going to call me back before you went to sleep?" I heard the annoying voice of Sharita. "You are sleep; I can hear it in your voice."

"Shut the fuck up." I told her. I sat up and yawned. She smacked her lips, and then huffed and puffed. I rolled my eyes and then left out of the room into the darkened hallway. I didn't know where I was going but I knew that I needed to find the kitchen before I was to die of hunger. I was on my way down the steps when I heard a door behind me open and a dim light come through. I turned around to see who was coming out of the room. It was a short petite girl name Mariah, who was only fifteen years old.

"Where is the kitchen?" I asked her as she approached me.

"It's down stairs and to the right." She informed me. Her voice was soft like a whisper. I followed her directions and found my way to the kitchen. I found me some ham and cheese and bread and made me a little sandwich. After I finished my sandwich at the breakfast nook I went downstairs into the family room and started watching television. The family room was separate from the living room; you weren't allowed in the living room. The family room was burgundy and tan. Tan sofas and love seats and walls and burgundy carpet; glass coffee table; flowers; fish tank; T.V. I was not sure of what the size was but it was big enough; and on the side of the couch was a photo album of off the kids that have ever lived in the house. There were a lot of kids, three books filled with pictures. I wondered why they never had kids of their own. I must have fell asleep because next thing I knew the T.V. cut off then I felt someone standing over me. I opened my eyes and saw Mr. Adams bending over me. He jumped back a little bumping into the coffee table.

"Oh damn, what time is it?" I asked while sitting up.

Mr. Adams looked at the VCR then turned and looked back at me, "Uh, 1:35," he said.

"Damn, I was sleep for a long ass time," I said. I swung my feet onto the floor and then began to rub my eyes. Mr. Adams sat beside me. "Let me go to my room." I said getting ready to get up and go. Mr. Adams grabbed my arm. I looked at him.

"Why you leaving so fast?" he asked me.

"Because I wanna go to my room; do you have a problem with that?" I asked him. He shook his head while saying. "Nah, but just sit down here with me for a couple of minutes to talk. You will be living under my roof now so you know I got to get to know you." He said to me. I sat back down and placed my hands on my lap. He turned facing me then licked his chocolate lips. "So how did you end up here?"

"Long story," I said.

"I have time,"

"Naw, that's Aiight. But um...Wassup with you and Mrs. Adams? Why you marry her?" I inquired being nosey.

"You tell me your story I'll tell you mine," I looked at him before going into my life story. I was surprised that I opened up to him and I hardly knew him, but I figured since he opened up his house to me I might as well inform him on what lead me here. After my story was told he began to get to his story, it wasn't much but it was a little something.

"Well, I didn't wanna marry her but then there was something about her that made me fall in love," he told me.

"Yeah right, you fell in love with her. As ugly as that woman is," I told him. He laughed one of the ugliest laughs I ever heard which turned me off, but when he made eye contact with me my turn-off became a turn-on. There was something about eyes that turned me on no matter how ugly a person is. But Mr. Adams was just sexy. We started talking and the whole time he had me laughing. He was thirty-eight and was funny, a painter and an architect, no kids, Ms. Adams couldn't have any kids due to early menopause, that's why they have this home for the kids. Trying to breath I said, "Hold up, hold up. You making my stomach hurt."

"You have a beautiful smile," he told me.

"Thank you," I laughed to myself. For what, I don't know. Then it got quiet and James, that's his real name, kept looking at me. "Where's the bathroom?" I asked breaking the silence.

"Uh, go down the hall and it's on your right."

I washed my hands and wiped them on a decorated towel in the bathroom, the ones that you're not suppose to use, there just up there to make the bathroom look nice but people use them anyway. I walked out the bathroom and cut the light back off. On my way back to the family room I noticed all the paintings on the wall they were beautiful. Majority of them were abstract paintings, didn't know what they mean but they where dark very dark, there were only I'll say two of them that were bright and looked like it was suppose to be someone's face. I looked at the artist name and my mouth fell open, James Adams. I was shocked that he could paint that well. I started walking back into the room when someone pulled me by my waist into the kitchen. Standing in front of me was James. He had me pent up against the refrigerator.

"Wassup," I said. He stared at me for a while not saying anything, and when I opened my mouth to say something he kissed me. I wanted to pull back but the kiss felt so good. I know it was wrong but I didn't have any going on a month, and that's not like me; I have to get some at least once a week. I knew he wanted me. They always do; the older men love them some young ones. Older women don't know what to do with these old dudes. I looked up at him and he looked down at me and kissed me again. Things were so intense we started having sex in the kitchen. He lifted me up on top of the counter and spread my legs as far as they would go, I quickly became moist knowing what was about to come. He lifted up my wife beater and exposed my B-cup breast; my coochie began to pulsate as he flicked his tongue over my hardened nipples. He then entered me, and began to pound into me, sex quickly filled the air. That was the best experience that I had until I heard someone come into the kitchen. I looked towards the doorway and saw Sharita standing there with a cynical look so I just leaned back and let my eyes wonder in the back of my head. He pumped one last and final time then pulled out; he pulled up his clothes and walked away. I fixed myself up and went to go upstairs when Sharita stopped me.

"Not even a whole day and you've already fucked James," Sharita said.

"Mind your damn business," I told her, then went upstairs and took a shower.

Chapter 5

Over the course of a month the sexcapade between James and I continued. Every chance we had alone together we made it our mission to fool around. I found myself spending more time with Quinton. He was so interesting to me. Every time I looked at him the sexual attraction that I had for him grew. Every time I was around I found me throwing myself at him, that was unusual for me because all I had to do was look at a boy and swing my hips a certain way and they would come crawling; but not in his case. It was hot out that day and stuffy in the house. Ms. Adams refused to turn on the AC unless it was a code red outside, so we had to suffer. All the windows in the house was open, the wind outside was blowing nothing but hot air into the house. Everyone was irritated. I lay on Quinton's bed with just my sports bra on. I fanned myself with a carryout menu that he had lying on his bed.

"Quinton, you don't have a fan in here?" I asked him. He was sitting in his chair drawing. He shook his head no. his chair was facing me. I noticed him keep looking at me. I didn't really pay it any attention until now. "Why do you keep looking at me?" I questioned. He didn't respond. I started to get up. "What are you over there drawing?"

"Lay back down, I'm almost finish," I did what he said. Ten minutes of just sitting there I began to get bored.

"Are you finished yet?" I asked a little annoyed.

"Yeah, you can move now," he told me with his face still plastered into his creation. I hopped off of the bed and over to him.

"Let me see," I tried to look, but he pushed me out of his way and continued to make the finishing touches. I stood back with one hand on my hips.

"Alright, I'm finish." He turned the picture around. A smile grew on my face.

"It's so pretty. Is it mine?" I asked him. The picture was a portrait of me lying on his bed. He caught every curve of my body. From the small sculpture of my breast, the well defined abs I obtained without trying, to the curves my hips possessed, and the voluptuous ass that I used to hypnotized my victims with.

"Yeah, I drew it for you." He told me. I leaned over and kissed him on his cheek. When I pulled back I looked him in his eyes and before he had a chance to move away I kissed him on his lips. His lips were soft and plump. I grabbed his face and parted his lips with my tongue. He pushed me back.

"Naw Nevaeh." he said.

I sighed. "What? Why are you acting like you don't want me?"

"Because I don't," he told me. I raised one of my eyebrows.

"What?" I asked more hurt than surprised.

"I'm gay." I took a step back away from him and scrunched up my face.

"You're what?" He sighed then smacked his lips.

"Nevaeh?" He tried to grab hold of my hand. I pulled it out of his grip. He put his head down. I didn't mean to hurt him I just didn't approve of homosexuality. We starred at each other for a while when his room door opened and in walked Sharita.

"Hey Quinton you seen," She stopped when she saw me. "I should've known you were in here. You're looking for some new dick to fuck. I'm sure Quinton wouldn't want your loose ass coochie." She said to me. "You know, you being passed around the whole Southern Ave already."

"Bitch, you need to shut your boney ass up before I shut you up!" I threatened coming towards her. Quinton stood up and grabbed me around my waist. Sharita laughed.

"Oh shut the fuck up. Some lil girl is downstairs looking for you." She looked at me again and chuckled, and then left closing the door behind her. I looked behind me at Quinton.

Nevaeh, talk to me." I tried to push his hand away from me but his grip was too tight. "Nevaeh?"

"Someone is downstairs waiting for me." I turned towards the door and he loosened his grip. Without giving him another look I grabbed my shirt off of his bed then walked out of his room and down the stairs.

I walked into the living room to come face to face with Janette. I hadn't seen her in a year maybe longer. She smiled when she seen me. Part of me wanted to hate her for not giving me some place to stay and the other half of me wanted to run and give her a big hug because she didn't forget about me. I walked up to her with my face frowned up. She still had a smile on her face.

"Hey boo," she said to me. I tried my hardest to give her an evil look but my heart just wouldn't let me. My frown slowly turned into a smirk which soon turned into a smile as I hugged her. Rocking back and forth we expressed to each other how much we missed one-an-other. Once we let go I slapped her on her arm.

"Trick, what you do that for?" She asked rubbing her arm.

"For not coming to see me sooner." I told her. She laughed. I motioned for her to follow me up to my room. "So wassup, what are you doing over here?" I asked her as I flopped down on my bed.

"What I can't come and see my best friend." I looked at her as I asked her what she wanted.

"Nothing, I just missed you. I wanted to check up on you and make sure you're alright." I nodded my head.

"Well as you can see I'm doing well. I can't complain, how is things going for you back at home?" She came and sat beside me on my bed.

"Well you know everything's been going good. My mamas suppose to be taking me one day this week to go and get my learners. I wanted you," She stopped when she seen the door swing open and Sharita came in yelling.

"No Kelvin, you said that you were gonna come over here! You always telling me that you're gonna do one thing but end up doing another. I'm tired of your bullshit!" She spat. Janette looked at me.

"Wassup with her?" She asked me. I shrugged my shoulders.

"I donno, the bitch got problems." We chuckled. Sharita cut her eyes at us.

"What was that?" She asked. I stopped laughing and became serious.

"I said you sitting over there whinnying, the dick aint that good."

"How you know?" Janette asked me. I knew what Janette was doing. She was being the instigator in the ordeal.

"Cause I fucked him like two nights ago. It's aright but it ain't good enough to be crying and shit over." Janette chuckled. I laughed right along with her. She knew that I was serious. I felt my head turn to the left and another blow come to my head knocking me back. I kicked

Sharita back and then stood up. "Bitch, have you lost your mother fuckin mind?" I went charging towards Sharita. We were giving it to each other. Our hands were tangled in each other hair. I swung her onto the floor and began banging her head onto the floor trying to get her away from my hair.

"Bitch get off her fuckin hair." I heard Janette yell. I seen a foot come towards us and hit Sharita up aside her head. After that first blow to the head I had seen one coming to her stomach.

"What the hell is all this yelling going on in here?" I heard Ms. Adams voice. I heard her run over to us and then felt her trying to pull us apart. "Nevaeh, let go of her hair. Nevaeh!" She shouted. "Quinton! James!" The next thing I know I was being pulled up off of the floor. We were still holding onto each other's hair. I let one of my hands free and swung on her three times, sending three blows to her head.

"Let her go Nevaeh," I heard Quinton tell me. He was trying to release my hands.

"Tell this bitch to let go of my hair first." I told him.

"Sharita." James said. I felt her loosening her grip from my hair. When I felt her let my hair go I gripped hers tighter then yanked her back to the floor. She cried out in pain. "Don't you ever come at me like that again! I should break your fuckin neck." I told her. I felt Quinton grip my waist tight.

"Let her go," he whispered in my ear.

"Ne-Ne, just let her go. You got her; just let her go before you get into some kind of trouble." The thought of me being kicked out and living back on the streets got to me. I released her from my grip. Quinton quickly grabbed me up and took me into his room. As I was leaving my room I heard the cries of Sharita and the yelling of Ms. Adams.

"Where is her case workers number? She has to go; I will not have that violence in my house." When we walked into Quinton's room he slammed the door shut leaving Janette on the other side out in the hallway. I walked over to his window and started to look out of it. I folded my arms over my tiny breast. He was quiet for a minute. I didn't have time to worry about what he was wondering. My main focus was on my living situation and how I was messing everything up. The bitch had it coming though.

"What the hell is wrong with you?" He asked me after a couple minutes of silence. I shrugged my shoulders not really wanting to talk about the situation at that point in time.

"What you mean you don't know?" He asked me, pressing for an answer. I looked at him.

"The bitch hit me first." I told him just a step from yelling. "I wasn't about to allow her to keep hitting me while my ass sit around lookin stupid." There was a knock at the door. He turned and opened the door and in came Janette.

"Who are you?" Quinton asked.

"Oh wassup, I'm Janette." She said extending her hand for a handshake. He took her hand in his. I looked at the way he looked at Janette like he wanted to rip her clothes off right there. I quickly became jealous.

"Don't even Janette, he's gay," The smirk that was on her face fell.

"Oh, well. That's a shame to let a good looking dude go to waste." She said to him looking him in the eyes. She bit her bottom lip showing that she was interested in him no matter his sexuality.

"Well how about I go get cleaned up and we can go to the mall Janette." She turned to me and said okay as she slipped her hand away from him. I put a frown on my face and walked through them and out the door.

Janette and I were walking Pentagon City Mall window shopping. Well she was window shopping. She refused for me to buy her anything; she was not the Janette I use to know. She usually accepted anything I gave her. I looked at her as we went into the store called Cache'. Her eyes lit up when she seen the beautiful clothes that they had to offer. I seen as she went over to this outfit the manikin was wearing and admired every piece of article it was wearing. I took notice of the things that she was admiring as we walked out of the store, I made a mental note to go back and pick up the things for her even though she told me not to. As we walked out I saw the last person I wanted to see. His name was Morris. Morris was about six foot even, held the frame of a football player, and a nice fade. I pulled Janette's arm to go the other way but it was too late, he was already calling my name and running up to me. I took a deep breath and turned facing him.

"What Morris?" I asked annoyed.

"Where the fuck have you been?" He asked me. I rolled my eyes and turned my head looking elsewhere.

"What do you want? I told you that I was through with you."

"Bitch, you still owe me money. I told you when you first got up with me that you don't leave my business until I say you leave." I licked my lips and put my hands on my hips.

"Nigga I don't owe you shit. You ain't never do anything for me, I got all my fuckin clients." I said with much attitude. I felt my body being yanked towards him. The look on my face showed him that I wasn't scared.

"Aye nigga, get your damn hands off of her." I heard Janette say as she tried pulling him away from me.

"While your ass out here spending my money you need to be in those streets spreading your legs." He looked over at Janette then back at me. "Keep fucking with my money and your friend over here gonna be planning a fuckin funeral for you." He pushed me away from him and then walked off. I stood in one spot trying to fix my clothes.

"Ne-Ne, what the hell was that?" I heard her ask. I tried to ignore her. She stood in front of me. "Nevaeh, what did you get yourself into?"

"I told you that you should've let me stay that night I came to your house. I wouldn't have ended up like this." I told her starring off in another direction instead of looking her in the eyes.

"Don't try and blame your hoeing on me. I told you to stop doing what you are doing, and you're still doing it. It's time that you settle your little ass down." She gave me a look that told me that she wasn't playing with me.

"Yeah, well settling my lil ass down don't put money in my pocket."

I told her then I walked away leaving her standing there looking at my back. I continued walking through the mall until my feet got tired. I admired all of the children that walked around the mall with their parents. I smiled as I seen the children pull their parents into the Disney store ready to play with all the gadgets the store had around for the children. I couldn't wait until I could experience those things with my children. I walked into the Disney store and began to look around. I was looking at the electronic train set when I felt something fall into the back of my leg. I turned around to see a little boy around the age of three sitting on the floor behind me. I bent down to meet him face to face.

"I'm sorry." He said to me. He was a cute little boy, dark chocolate with little dreads growing already.

"It's okay," I looked down and seen him playing with a little action figure. I smiled at him; he was so into his toy that he didn't notice I was still looking at him. I touched him on the top of his head then stood up. I grabbed the train set that I was looking at and paid for it. I went to one more store before I left the mall then headed to the love of my life's house before I went back to the group home.

I walked up the stairs and into my room placing my bags on the floor beside my bed. I flopped down on my bed tired, but I knew I couldn't go to sleep just yet because I had another mission to do. I leaned back on my bed and closed my eyes. I thought about all of the shit that I had been through and all the shit I see myself getting into in the feature. I felt myself drifting off so I sat up. I had the urge to get up and talk to Quinton. I yawned as I made my way to his room. I heard laughter when I reached his room the laugh of Janette. I opened his door a little. Again I heard Tupac's poetic lyrics blaring. I opened the door a little more. My eyes widened as I seen the two tonguing each other down.

"Spying are we?" I jumped and then slammed his door shut. I turned around and seen Ms. Cummings standing behind me.

"No." I said moving around her. I walked into my room with her right behind me. I sat on my bed and she sat on a chair that we had in the room. "So what, are you taking me somewhere else?" I asked her.

"No. I came to see what happened. I received a call from Terri telling me you whooped Sharita's ass."

"Sharita hit me first." I let her know.

"Why?"

"Because she got mad cause I said that her boyfriend is no one to be crying over because the dick ain't that good." She shook her head with a grin on her face. I put one on mine as well.

"How do you know that? Did you have sex with him?"

"Yup, and I told her. I told her that it was okay but not to be cryin over. She can find better dick to be cryin over." She chuckled.

"You are extremely free with your sexual accouters."

"Why be ashamed? Its human, don't sit and act like you don't do it." We sat and we talked. I never realized how much I can open up to one person, which was a first to me. I never opened up to anyone before; except Janette. I think it was because she seemed caring, she was beautiful, and young. While we talked and joked around I unpacked my clothes. I pulled the toy train out of its bag.

"That's for your little boy down at the home?" She asked me. The home was a foster home for younger children. I smiled.

"Yeah, he'll be one in two months."

"That's right July 20th. It looks like someone else's birthday is coming up in two weeks as well." I smiled again. "So what do you wanna do for your birthday?"

"I don't know. I never got anything for my birthday so I'm not looking forward to anything. Just to be healthy." She nodded her head.

"So how is school?"

"Besides having fifty million tutors, and trying to catch up on this tenth grade work it's very hard. I mean I'm catching on but my main problem is I'm still having trouble reading."

"Bout time you got back." I looked to the door and seen Janette walking in. She looked at Ms. Cummings and stopped in her tracks. "I'm sorry, do I need come back?"

"No sweetie, you're okay. Nevaeh, call me later we'll talk about that problem okay." I nodded my head. She left. Janette came and sat on the same chair that Ms. Cummings just got up from. I looked at her. I was so jealous of her. The family that loved her, the way she respected her body, the inner beauty that she had, and the intelligence that kept her ahead.

"Are you still mad at me?" I shook my head. "Good cause I have something to tell you. Let me tell you about Quinton."

"He fuck you good?" I asked. She gave me this confused look.

"What? I didn't fuck him." She told me.

"Didn't look like that to me when I went to his room. Ya'll was tonguing each other down, I'm surprised you can still talk."

"Okay, yeah we did kiss but we didn't," she paused then she twisted her head to the side and looked at me. "Is this the reason why you are mad at me? You think I want to fuck him?" I didn't respond. "Ne-Ne, I've never fucked anyone and I would never fuck someone I just met. I am not a whore. So for you to think I would do something like that hurts. I don't want his ass. You can have him. Especially if this is gonna make you mad at me." Tears swelled in her eyes. I felt bad. I listened to her get on me. I attempted to say something to her but she shot me down.

"So that's what you think of me, a hoe, because I needed money to survive? I helped your ass when we were out on the streets. I could've kept that money to myself and left you ass out." I argued.

"I appreciate what you did for me, but you don't have to do what you are doing for me." She told me. I sighed. I told myself that I wasn't going to cry, I refused to let people see how they hurt me. I reached over the side of my bed and pulled out a Cache' bag and handed it to her.

"What is this?" She asked me.

"It's yours. Now if you would excuse me I have things to do." I told her as I stood up. She looked at me when I left out my room. I went into the bathroom and started the shower. When I walked back into the room she was gone. I took my shower and left headed over to the foster home to visit my baby.

After I left the home that night I went walking the streets. I found myself on Fourteenth Street in DC with all the rest of the prostitutes. That's where I received most of my clients. That night I had sex with six or seven men making almost five hundred. Seventy-five dollars a fuck is what I charged. My extra short jean mini skirt and yellow tube top made it easier for my clients' trynna get their quick nut before they had to return home to their stressful lives. I was on my way to the bus stop when a black 94' Mercedes Benz rolled up beside me. I looked into the car as the windows rolled down. It was Morris.

"Get in." I sucked my teeth and kept walking. I was about to walk across the street when he pulled in front of me pointing a 9mm in my face. "Get your ass in the car." With no second thought I hopped into his car. We rode in his car but we were going the opposite way of my house.

"Come on Morris, I gotta get home."

"Why you wanna go back there? What was wrong with you staying with me?"

"Morris, please take me home." We pulled up to Forest Creek apartments. Tears began to swell in my eyes. "Please, I just came out here to make your money. I told you earlier that I was through with this life style once I get you your money." I told him. Tears started to slip down my cheek. I looked him in his eyes as he ran his hand through my hair, then I felt my head being thrown back with his hand pulling my hair.

"Ahh!" I screamed

"Who you fucking at that damn house?"

"No, no one." I cried.

"You gotta be fucking someone for you to wanna stop."

"I just wanna get my life together. I have to get Jaquile, so I have to get my life together."

"Fuck Jaquile! You don't stop doing this shit until I say you can stop fucking these niggas out here. You got me?" I tried to close my mouth to muffle my cries and nodded my head. "That's a good girl. Now wipe your eyes so you can go up there and please those niggas." I did as he said. I wiped my face then went upstairs and opened my legs to at least four different dudes. When I walked outside Morris was gone. I sighed. I walked down the street to a gas station and used the pay phone. I called the first person who I thought would come and get me.

"Hello," I heard one of the kids say in a sleepy tone.

"Sharita, can you please wake Quinton up?" I begged of her.

"It's two o'clock in the morning. Call him back tomorrow."

"Please Sharita, its Nevaeh. Please wake him up for me." I began to cry. "I need help." I heard Sharita get up.

"Quinton, Quinton get up, telephone."

"Who the fuck is callin me at two in the morning?" Quinton ask annoyed.

"Nevaeh, she talking about she needs help."

"Yeah?" Quinton said into the receiver.

"Please come and get me, I'm at the gas station by Forest Creek." I cried.

"Why, never mind, I'll be there in ten minutes." He told me before he hung up. Those ten minutes seemed more like thirty minutes. I stood beside the service counter waiting for him. There wasn't many people coming to the gas station this time of night but there was a group of boy sitting at the entrance of the neighborhood. I was scared sitting out there alone. Morris never left me before. I was in worst situations, but I never fucked around with men like the ones that were around that neighborhood like that. I was trying to get my life together, but it was hard when Morris was keeping me hostage.

I began to make my way over to the payphone, ready to call Quinton back. I knew that being out in these cold streets was not where I wanted to be. Yes, I did live in the streets my whole life. I wanted to be better than what I was becoming, but it was hard when the streets were all I knew. Opening my legs for every stranger to walk by was my job. I put in extra overtime every day, only to be fucked over by greedy niggas who won't just accept one nut. My thighs were sore, my insides were tied in knots, and my heart only had two more pieces left to be broken before it tumbled down from heartache and pain. 'Beeep' 'Beeep'. "Neaveh, come on." Quinton voice brought me out of my daydream. I quickly walked over to the car and got in. not one word was said between the both of us as we made our way home.

Chapter 6

The next day I acted like nothing happened the day before, the fight between Sharita and me, the argument with me and Janette, the fact that Quinton told me that he was gay and the confrontation with Morris. I walked around the house quiet, kind of zombie like. I was ready to leave this place already. I knew the people inside didn't like me. I knew they knew what I was doing, and if it was before Janette came back in my life I wouldn't care what they thought of me. I wanted to show her that I was better than what she thought of me. I had to prove to everyone around me that I could take care of myself as well as the people who came into my life. I kept to myself for two months.

I barley stayed in the room when Sharita came in, for the simple fact I knew my mouth and attitude. If she said something or looked at me the wrong way Lord knows what I would've been capable of doing to her. I couldn't take the risk of another confrontation between us. Even though I had stopped having sex with niggas that I didn't know, it didn't stop me and James from continuing our affairs. I snuck down to his office three days a week while everyone in the house was asleep. Other times when I was not with him I would walk past his office and hear him and Sharita. Some days they would be arguing about the time that he and I had spent together. Times I would receive calls from Morris. He would leave me messages on my voice mail telling me how he was going to kill me because I was his property and I owed him money. I tried to ignore him, and for two months I did. I remember I was sitting in my room reading 'The Coldest Winter Ever' by Sista Souljah when I was interrupted by someone entering the room. I looked up from my reading and seen Janette standing by the door. I rolled my eyes at her and then looked back down at my book.

"Shouldn't you be up in the room with your lil boo?" she sucked her teeth.

"I know you are not still mad at that shit. I told you before, I don't want him. If you want him you can have him." I sighed loudly, letting her know that I was bored with her. I wasn't mad I just didn't know what to say to her.

"You gonna let some nigga come in between our friendship?" I looked at her. She was all that I had. There were plenty of times when she got on my nerves and I couldn't let that one time make me get rid of my only friend.

"You been coming over here for the past month, but not once did you come in here and try to talk to me." I sat up giving her room to sit down on the bed.

"I was only coming over because Quinton said he really needed someone to talk to."

"Umm." Was the only response I gave.

"He told me how he thought he could talk to you, but you dissed him after he told you that he was gay. That nigga ain't really gay; he said that he was slowly falling in love with you, but he knows that he couldn't have you."

"Who said that he couldn't have me? I've been basically throwing myself at him since I got here." Janette chuckled as she nodded her head.

"Go ask him why he can't have you. He wanted me to come in here to tell you that he needed to talk to you anyways." I sat in my room for ten more minutes listening to Janette talk before I went to Quinton's room. I knocked on his door and waited for him to tell me it was okay for me to go in. when he told me to come in I walked in and shut the door behind me. Quinton turned around in his chair and looked at me.

"Wassup." I sat on his bed.

"Janette said you wanted to talk to me." He nodded his head, but didn't say anything. We sat there quiet for a couple of seconds. "So what did you wanna talk to me about?"

"I'm not gay."

"Okay, so why did you tell me that you were?"

"Because that was the only way I knew that I could keep you from tryna fuck me."

"Okay so tell me why you don't wanna have sex with me. Am I ugly or what?"

"Nah, you're far from ugly. If I could I'd bun you up, make you forget about all these other niggas you messing with."

"Then why can't you do that?" he didn't say anything. "Hello?"

"Because I have AIDS." He blurted out. A cold chill went throughout my body. AIDS. I knew it was out there but I didn't think I would ever meet anyone with the deadly disease. He didn't look sick.

"You're lying to me again, if you're already messing with someone that's all you had to say. You know how many other niggas is out there waiting for me?" he looked at me.

"Do you know how stupid you sound?" I stood up to leave. He jumped in front of me. "I was born with this shit. I'm still a fuckin virgin. I never been with a female or a nigga. My muva was out doing the same shit you're doing, fucked my life up for materialistic shit.
Since you moved in here five months ago I wanted to be with you physically and mentally. For real I just wanted you to be a damn friend and understand where I'm coming from. I know the stuff you out here doing Nevaeh and I know almost every nigga you had sex with. The streets talk." He told me. I looked at him in the eyes. He was pleading for me to be his friend through his eyes. I held my arms out to him, not because I felt sorry for him but because I wanted to have him close to me. It was hard for me to admit it at first, but I was falling for him like he was for me and we couldn't have each other.

Quinton and I spent every waking hour together. He became my human diary. He listened to every problem that I had without judging me. It was hard and very tempting to be with him knowing that I was attracted to him sexually. He helped me catch up with school. Summer time came and I had to go to summer school. I knew when I decided to go back to school I had to go through summer school to catch up. Quinton picked me up every day from school. It was one day that I wish he never picked me up. Then I wouldn't have gone back to the life that I was trying to leave behind.

I was sitting on the hand rail in front of the school waiting for Quinton to arrive. He was late picking me up; it didn't worry me because he was always late. On that particular day I felt something wrong was going to happen. It was eighty-five degrees out with a slight breeze. I felt like an ant underneath of a magnifying glass. A thin sundress barely covered my body. My hair was in a bun making my neck visible to the sun. There was an eerie silence for awhile and then Biggie Smalls 'Hypnotize' blared from down the hill. I stayed seated text messaging Janette until the 95' black impala became visible and parked. I watched as Morris stepped out of the car. I walked over to him, and stood a good distance away from him.

"You can't answer my phone calls now." His Channel sun glasses hid his eyes.

"What do you want?" he opened up the passenger side door.

"Get in."

"Excuse you?" I asked.

"Get in the car so you can go and make my money."

"I don't do that shit anymore." I said proudly.

"Bitch please, who got you talking like that? That nigga Quinton, He ain't taking care of you, got you out here looking like a two dollar hooker. That cheap shit you got on. Come on so daddy can take care of you." Something inside of me wanted to go with him and return to my old life. I heard tires screeching followed by the slamming of a door.

"Nevaeh get in the car." I moved away from Morris car and over to Quinton's. "Get in the car." He told me again as he passed me. He got into Morris face. I stood by the car wanting to interject.

"Stay the fuck away from her, if I find out you been near her I'm gonna fuck all your shit up. You got me?"

"Yeah aight." Quinton turned to walk away. Morris was letting him walk away too easy and that was not like him. Quinton was almost to the car when multiple shots rang out. Quinton stopped right where he was standing and dropped to the ground. I was stuck, my body wouldn't move, my eyes wouldn't cry, and my voice box wouldn't let me scream. The world had stopped. Morris was still standing by his car with a grin on his face. I then knew how my mother felt when my daddy died right in front of her. The police sirens made everything move again. Morris hopped in his car and tried to drive off but the police blocked him in. while I was text messaging Janette I told her that Morris showed up, and I told her to call me in five minutes, if I didn't answer the phone then call the police. Paramedics rushed over to Quinton's lifeless body. Before the police had a chance to question me I disappeared into the woods.

"Nevaeh, Nevaeh stop running." I ran down an alley into a dead end. I stomped my foot in frustration. "I see you went back to the street life." I turned around to face Ms. Cummings. The only clothes my body wore were a blue spandex tub top dress and black stiletto heels. My hair hung over my face, covering up a fresh bruised eye. I was back on the streets because I had no place to go. I knew they didn't want me back at that house after all the drama I had caused.

"Just let me be, It's my fault Quinton is dead. The Adams don't want me back in their house.

"How do you know that?"

"Cause I brought too much drama in that house."

"You let me worry about them. Come on so we can get you cleaned up and some place cooler." When she got close up on me a look of concern was written on her face. "What happened?" I turned my head away from her and wrapped my arms around myself.

"I got into some trouble with this guy I met."

"A guy like that Morris dude?"

"He said that he would take care of me. He said that he wasn't going to treat me like Morris did."

"Is he still making you have sex with all these different men in one day?"

"He isn't making me do anything that I don't wanna do." She did a sarcastic laugh.

"Nevaeh, get in the car."

"No, I like it out in the cold."

"Don't you want to get your son back?" My bottom lip began to tremble. It felt like pins were sticking me in my throat as I told her,

"He's better off in that place. Maybe someone will adopt him into a nice home and give a much better life than I had and that I could supply." Tears were falling from my eyes. "Excuse me, I have clients." I walked around her and back down the alley into the main streets.

Life was going okay for awhile. I had everything under control as long as I did everything Mike had asked of me. I always told myself that I wouldn't become a man's footstool, but when he gets me whatever I want the least I could do is abide by his rules. One day while I was out standing on the corner when a black 1998 Ford Expedition pulled up beside me. I walked up to the car and leaned into it. My tub top dress showed off a sample of my ass.

"What's up?" I asked the cute man inside of the car.

"I'm tryna bust off this quick nut." He told me.

"Mmmh, I can help you with that." I said, and then I got into his car. Before I had a chance to get comfortable I was being read my rights. I had been booked for soliciting, so embarrassing. When I had gotten down to the police department they had placed me in a holding cell. They made me sit in a small hole in the box with little or no room to move with people who did worst things then soliciting. I sat in the cell for two hours before they processed me into the system. They gave me a warning because I was still a minor and it was my first time; but they didn't just let me go on my own they had me call someone to pick me up. The only person I thought would come and pick me up was Ms. Cummings. When she came she looked so pissed off at me. When they released me she didn't wait inside the station for me, she just went sat in her car. The whole ride she didn't say a word.

Chapter 7

"Ay Girl." a boy yelled. Janette and I were walking through Iverson mall. Three months had passed since Quinton had died and I had just stopped having nightmares about that day. "Aye girl." I turned around to see who was yelling. I usually don't turn around because for ONE my name isn't 'Ay girl' or 'Showdy' or 'Black shirt' or whatever color I'm wearing that day. For TWO if a male wanted to come talk to me he need to come at me and ask for my name politely and maybe, just maybe I may consider giving it to him depending on if he's cute. It was Key Shawn and Brandon; they were in one of my classes. I caught up in school and even made honor roll once or twice. I realized that I was smart as shit when it came to books, but as far as niggas I was dumb as hell. I blame mama for that one.

"Wassup Shawn, Brandon," I said.

"Hey girl. What you doing up here?" Key Shawn asked, licking his half-black, half-pink lips. I would love to see how he tastes, I thought to myself.

"What do you do at the mall?"

"Aight, ain't gotta sass me." I smiled at him. Janette elbowed me in my side. I looked at her and she darted her eyes towards Brandon.

"Brandon this is Janette, Janette this is Brandon." Brandon was the color of a freshly baked chocolate chip cookie. He stood two inches shorter than Key'Shawn at five-foot-eight, with a mini bush.

"Wassup," Brandon said.

"Nothin, wassup with you?" Janette said blushing.

"Aight can ya'll carry on ya'll conversation over there." I more like told them pointing over by the escalator. Janette rolled her eyes at me and sucked her teeth. I rolled my eyes back at her playfully. "Come on." They walked over to a bench and sat down.

"Anyway, I was getting some clothes, what about you?" I questioned him.

"I'm 'bout to go get me some shoes." We were talking about school and everything we could think of for the last fifteen minutes and everything was going good when he said.

"So yeah, I ain't even going to fake all I'm tryna do is, yeah you know." To tell the truth that's all I wanted to do with him, but in order for him to get what he wanted I had to get what I wanted. I learned that from mama too, she always had sex with men to get whatever she wanted, so I had figured it was okay. I moved up close to Key' Shawn pushing my body against his, making sure my breast is all up on him. I leaned in to whisper in his ear and I felt his warm breath on the nape of my neck making my knees get weak. I couldn't really get up close to him so I stood close enough and talked to him a sexy whisper. I placed my hands around his neck.

"Aight, well how bout you buy me this purse. Doesn't matter what color; just make sure it's Coach, and this jump-suit outfit from out of Mchunu. Then call me and I'll meet you at your place and we'll do whatever you want," I leaned back waiting to see what he would say.

"Aight," he took his pager off his waist and handed it to me. "Just take this. I'mma page you and tell you when to come," he informed me.

"Aight," I said. He was dumb, but there was no doubt he was fine. I knew him well enough to know he was not the type of boy that I would carry on a relationship with, but the one I would just drag along. I was on the lookout for the bad boy/ mama boy type of dude. You know the kind that don't give a fuck but love his mama, will do anything for her, and respect the females; one that doesn't have a problem with doing whatever he has to do to survive. One that was like my daddy, the way my mama described him. That's not afraid to argue with his girl, and let her win sometimes but not all the times. I'm not looking for them dudes that say that they go hard but are some punks, ones that will constantly lie, and has no type of goal in life, or job, and HUSTLIN' IS NOT A JOB. I called over to Janette to tell her to come on then went back to shopping.

After leaving the mall Janette and I went to the shelter and spent some time with Jaquile. After the visit Janette and I went our separate ways. I went home that evening and put my clothes on my bed. On my way down to the kitchen I heard some noise coming from out of the downstairs rooms. I pushed open the door and what I saw made me want to throw-up. Sharita was down on her knees while James was sitting on the chair in front of her; she was downing his cum like she dehydrated. That was something I would never do. I couldn't watch her doing what she was doing so I closed the door back and went into the living room and started watching television. Fifteen minutes later she came out wiping her mouth off and sat beside me picking up the phone.

"Put it in your mouth," I said making fun of her. She looked at me with evil eyes then back at the phone and began pressing numbers. I laughed and continued watching T.V.

"Wassup boo?" Sharita said into the phone. She stayed on the phone and the bad part was, she was always talking about nothing, ever since I started living there. I didn't want to hear what she was going to talk about so I went up to the room, put my clothes away and took a nap.

Beeeep, Beeeep Beeeep Beeeep. "What the hell is that noise?" I asked aggravated with my eyes closed and my head under the pillow. The beeping sound kept going off after two minute pause so I lifted up my head and looked at my nightstand. It was the pager that Key Shawn gave me two weeks ago. I looked at time displayed on the pager; it was 1:30 am. I read the number that came through then called the number back.

"Hello," I said into the phone.

"Come over now," I heard a male say into the phone. I tried to make out the voice but I couldn't.

"Who's this?" I asked.

"Who you think?" He quizzed me.

"Key Shawn?" I said unsure.

"Yeah."

"Man, nigga it's two o'clock in the morning, what do you want?"

"Come over here," he told me.

"For what?" I asked.

"To come get your shit."

" Oh, where you live?" He gave me the address and I hung up.

"Where you going?" Sharita questioned me. She was sitting up in her bed wide awoke. I did not know her like that to tell her my business.

"You all in my business like I like you, take your ass back to sleep." I told her. She sucked her teeth and crossed her arms. I see why she be needs to suck someone's dick, she need some attention. I went and took a quick shower and put on my pink night shorts and white tank top, with half my ass sticking out the shorts. I had that Jennifer Lopez body, big ass, little titties, but it was cool though, the niggas wasn't complaining. I walked down the stairs and snuck out of the house without making a sound. When I reached his house I saw cars in the driveway. I paid the cab driver then got out and walked up to his averaged size house and knocked on the door. He answered the door with just his jeans on. His body had made me want to jump on him and have my way with him right in the doorway.

"Come in," he said quietly. I walked into his house and began observing my surroundings. The stairs were straight ahead, but in the hallway were family pictures. He looked exactly like his mama and little sister. "Your stuff is in my room," he said as he pushed me to the back of the house and down some steps. His room was in the basement; his room was like a regular boy room. From what I've known his family was wealthy, his mom was a lawyer and his dad was a police officer. He took a bag off his bed and handed it to me. I looked in the bag and seen a black purse, black-jump suit with the words Mchunu on it and a tennis bracelet. Key Shawn came closer to me and put his hands around my waist. "Aiight now that you got what you wanted plus something extra, can I get what I want?" I dropped the bag and didn't hesitate to kiss him. We were on the bed and each piece of our clothing was thrown someplace in the room. He explored my whole body with his tongue; he ate like it was going to be his last meal making, me have multiple orgasms. He came back up and protected himself and went in me. About ten minutes into it things were just heating up when, "I'm bout to cum," Key Shawn said. I looked at him with a disgusted look on my face. He rolled off of me and fell asleep.

"Oh my goodness," I said. Now I knew he wasn't the type of dude I could mess with. He couldn't even stay up long enough for me to enjoy. I went back home to Ms. Adams sitting by the door waiting for me. She scared me when I walked past the living room and she was sitting in the chair with a not so bright light on. I tried to walk past her and up the stairs, but she stopped me.

"Where were you?" Ms. Adams asked me standing up.

"Over one of my friend's house."

"I am trying to help you out. I didn't have to take you back into my house. So don't disrespect it. Don't be leaving out this house at wee hours of the night."

"Whatever. Like you said you didn't have to take me back in. So now you gotta deal with the shit I bring." I ran up the stairs.

Chapter 8

A week before my birthday I found out Sharita was eighteen and it was time for her to go. I was happy that she was leaving because I thought I was going to be having a room all to myself but instead there was a ten-year-old girl they decided to take in. I loved little kids but I have never shared a room with one before. Ms. Adams began to get suspicious about all of the things that I was getting without a job. She knew my about my past life but she didn't know that I was at it again. I wasn't really sleeping with a lot of dudes like I was it was just Key'Shawn. The thing was he was getting me the stuff, as long as I give him what he wants, I'll get what I want.

"Nevaeh can you do my hair like yours?" Angel asked me. Angel was the little girl I had to share a room with. She was so pretty with long thick hair, copper skin, hazel cat shaped eyes, long beautiful legs. She ran for the track team at school, she was going to be the next Flo Joe. She sat down in front of me and I twisted her hair going back. I finished her hair then went and sat on the front porch. There was a new boy moving in that day. He was tall paper sack skin, long braids, hazel eyes and a killer smile. I sat on the first step as he walked back and forth from the house to the car that dropped him off. He made his last visit to the car then came and sat down beside me.

"Wassup," he said. His voice was deep and sexy.

"Hey." I said shyly. That what was all said when Ms. Adams came out.

"Nevaeh come and clean this kitchen up." I rolled my eyes.

"Aight, I'll be in there when I finish her hair." I did the last two twists and then got up and went in the house. I began washing dishes and singing to myself when I felt someone come behind me and wrap their arms around me. "Girl you know i-i-i-i love you." James sound trying to sound likes Lenny Wilkins. I laughed at how bad he sounded. "You still mess with that Shawn boy?" He asked me.

"Yeah, why?"

"No reason. You gonna come to my office later tonight when your mom go to sleep?"

"Yeah," I turned around facing him. "That winch is making me clean up the kitchen." I pouted.

"Give me a kiss." he said.

"Why? You gonna make us get caught,"

"No I'm not, just give me a kiss." I leaned forward kissing him, things got intense and he started rubbing on me.

"Nevaeh." a male said. I released from the kiss and turned to see who called me. It was the new boy standing in the doorway. I pushed James away from me. I did not want the boy to know what be going on between James and I. "There is this boy who wants you in the living room,"

"Oh Aight." I went into the living room with the boy following me, he went and sat on the couch watching me the whole time I went up to Key Shawn and he handed me three hundred dollars and said. "Be at my house tonight around ten,"

"I can't tonight," I told him.

"Why not?" He asked.

"Because I have something to do."

"What you doing tonight?"

"Damn, none of your business, I'll just come and see you the day after tomorrow; Friday."

"Aight whateva, can I get a kiss from my girl before I leave?" Key Shawn said.

"Oh, so I'm your girl now?" I asked confused. When did we ever establish this? I never agreed to that.

"Yeah, give me a kiss," he forcefully pulled me into a kiss. I pulled back and looked at him. He looked over at the boy that was sitting on the couch.

"Wassup," Key Shawn said. The boy nodded his head then turned around; Key Shawn gave me another kiss on my cheek then left the house.

I called Janette around eight that evening and told her about the new boy and how cute he was. She said she was going to be right over to see what he looked like and what he was all about, then hung up the phone. I stayed upstairs for a while reading a poem "Will You Ever Know My Soul" by Billye Okera, my favorite poet. I always dreamed in being a poet, I was determined to make it one day.

I finished reading the poem and put the book back under my pillow. I went downstairs and sat on the couch and started watching T.V. with the boy. I picked up the remote off the table and put the T.V. on mute, he turned and looked at me and said, "Aye man turn the T.V. up,"

"Naw I wanna talk to you for a minute," I told him.

"I don't wanna talk,"

"You wanted to talk earlier," I reminded him.

"That was earlier,"

"Well can you at least tell me your name?"

"Jermaine,"

"Well Jermaine, come here and sit by me," I said patting the seat next me.

He looked at the seat then at me. "Naw, I'm aight,"

"Okay, well how did you end up in here?" I asked him.

"Didn't I just tell your ass I ain't feel like talkin," he looked straight at me then turned and looked back at the television. "Turn the T.V. back up," he told me. I sat the remote down on the couch and went to the bathroom.

When I returned from the bathroom, I saw Janette in the living room trying to flirt with Jermaine. I stood in the doorway while they sat on the couch not knowing I was in the room. She was all over him so he moved over and said,

"Come on now you're like two-year old."

She giggled. "Shut up," Janette didn't look like she was two but she did look like she was nine or ten. I started giggling to myself; they turned and looked at me.

"Wassup Nevaeh," Janette said.

"Not a damn thing,"

"Oh," she turned and looked at Jermaine. "So you gonna come with me to the movies to night?"

Jermaine thought about it for a second then said, "Naw, maybe next time, I got something to do tonight,"

"Aiight," he turned his head back around and started watching T.V.

"Janette," I said. She turned around and I mouthed to her, "That's my man."

She rolled her eyes and said, "Whateva, I thought your man was Key Shawn,"

"Girl please, he *THINKS* he's my man,"

"I'll see ya'll lata," Jermaine said as he got up and walked away.

"Man, why you tryna get at him? Don't you have Brandon?" I said to her.

"Don't you have James and Key Shawn," she said to me.

"So fuckin what, now I want Jermaine."

She sucked her teeth, "Anyway, he's not my type, you can have him," Janette said. We sat and talked about Key Shawn and Jermaine and Brandon.

Janette went home around nine o'clock. I didn't have anything to do so I called Key Shawn up and told him I was on my way and I got ready to go over there. I walked downstairs getting ready to go call a cab when I seen Jermaine bout to walk out the door.

"Jermaine," I said as I walked up behind him. He jumped and turned towards me.

"What?" He said.

"Where you're going?" I asked him.

"Out,"

"Well can you take me over my friend house, you don't have to pick me up," he looked at me and I said, "Please," I said begging.

"Aight, come on," We left out the house and got into his black Crown Vic with tents. When he first pulled off everything was quiet between us; the only thing you could hear was Backyard blasting from the speakers. When he got about a block from our house I turned the music down. He looked at me and turned it back up. I turned it back down.

"Leave my radio alone," he told me.

"Why you so mean to me?" I asked him.

"You're irritating," he told me.

"How come you won't talk to me?" I asked him again.

"What do you want to talk about?" He questioned me.

"Tell me about yourself,"

"What do you want to know?"

"Everything,"

He looked at me then back at the road, "Aiight, well I'm seventeen, have no brothers or sisters..." He told me his whole life story, he was exactly what I was looking for except he didn't have a job, but he did do his little dirt on the side. I had to find some way to get with him. I noticed we had some things in common. His dad died when he was young, but the cause was cancer, and both of our mothers were alcoholics and crack addicts. He was taken during school by social services and placed under the custody of the government. I looked up to see where we were; we were sitting parked in front of Key Shawn's house.

"Do you know him?" I looked at Jermaine and asked.

"Know who?" He asked me back.

"Key Shawn,"

"Naw, why?"

"Cause I never told you where he lived,"

"Well yeah, I do know him, but were not exactly friends,"

"Oh, Aiight. Well I'll see you later on tonight or tomorrow,"

"Aiight," I got out the car and watched him sped off down the street.

I didn't make it home until the next morning. When I got there I had to hear Mrs. Adams mouth about me being out all night long. She told me that she had warned me last time when I had left out late at night; she was about to call Mrs. Cummings, but James told her con't do that, but it wasn't like I was going to stay in the house if she did. After they preached to me for about an hour I went upstairs to take a shower, and then went to sleep.

I woke up about an hour later to see Angel and her friends standing in the middle of the floor practicing cheers.

"No, it don't go like that! You gotta put your hands up first," one of the little girls yelled.

"Shh, you gonna wake her up," Angel said.

"It's okay; I'm already up," I said as I got up. I went to the bathroom, and on my way out I bumped into Jermaine.

"You just getting in?" I asked him.

"Naw, I got in last night, about two hours after I dropped you off."

"Oh,"

"I see you were out all night. Did you have fun?" He asked me as he began to walk to his room with me following behind him.

"Not really," I told him.

"Why not?" We made it to his room and he sat on his bed and I stood in front of him.

"Because," I said as I pushed him on the bed. I got on top of him and said. "I didn't get to 'do' who I wanted to 'do'." I got real close to him and looked in to his eyes.

"You still can't *'do'* who you want to *'do'*," Jermaine told me.

"Why not?" I asked him.

"Cause, you already 'doing' too many people. Now excuse me," he pushed me off of him and I landed next to him. He got up and left the room.

"Ugh..."

I fixed my clothes then got up and walked out the room. I walked downstairs to James office and seen him painting, I walked into the room and sat on his desk.

Without looking at me he said, "I thought you said you were going to come down here last night?"

"Oh, I forgot. I'm sorry. I'll come down here tonight, around twelve," I told him.

"You better be down here," he said in a tone that I have never heard him use before.

"I'm going to be down here." I hoped off his desk and walked out his office. I went upstairs and took yet another shower, and put on some tight fitted jeans and a red shirt. Sitting on my bed putting on my shoes I looked over at Angel watching T.V. "Angel, you wanna go with me to the mall?" I usually don't take anyone out with me when I go to the mall, because they might see something they like and expect me to get it for them, but I got tired of watching Angel's sad face when I tell her no she can't go with me. She was the only one in the house under the age of fifteen and I know she got tired of being in the house all the time. All her little friends were gone and it was just her in the room in front of the T.V. watching Ms. Doubtfire, the toys were still all over the floor.

"Yeah, I wanna go," she said as she jumped up.

"Aiight, turn off the T.V. and come on." She did what I said then walked behind me out the room.

"Jermaine guess where we going," she said as I turned around and seen her jump into Jermaine's arms. He acted like he was about to pick her up off the ground but he didn't. They laughed.

"Where are ya'll going?" He asked.

"To the mall," she told him.

"You are?"

"Yeah, can you take us?"

"I donno, I got something to do shorwdy,"

"Please, I don't wanna take the bus,"

"Uh..." She put on this cute little sad face. Jermaine laughed and said, "Aiight, I'll take ya'll."

"You gonna shop with us too!" Angel asked excited.

"I donno, but right now let's get you to the mall," Jermaine carried Angel to the car on his back with me behind them. Angel hopped off of his back and got into the back seat as he walked around the front and got into the driver seat and I got in the passenger side, then he pulled off in complete silence. Jermaine was only here for two days, but it seems like him and Angel knew each other forever. Their chemistry was just so strong.

"Can you turn on the radio please?" Angel asked. Jermaine and I both reached for the radio when our hands rubbed up against each other; he quickly snatched his hand away from mines as if I had some contagious disease. I looked at him and continued to turn on the radio. A boy has never acted that way towards me, anything they wanted to be more close to me.

We made it to the mall within fifteen minutes, to my surprise he got out and went in with us. He took Angel into KB Toys and brought her whatever she wanted, he didn't say a word to me and I started to feel uncomfortable thinking if it was what I said earlier. We took turns going into stores, I tried to buy Angel something but he wouldn't let me, so while they went into "Limited Too!" I sat outside the store looking at everybody that walked in and out of the store. I must have been in deep thought because I didn't even hear Jermaine calling my name. I turned and looked at him; he had like twenty bags in his hands.

"Watch her while I go to the bathroom and take these bags to the car."

"Aiight we gonna be over there at the bookstand," I said while standing up.

"Aiight," he walked off and he walked over to the bookstand. I was looking at a book called "Thugs and The Women That Love Them", I was thinking about getting it when Angel came up to me showing me a book.

"Can you buy this for me please?" She asked handing me a book. I took the book and said okay. I didn't know she read books, I always thought no child her age like to read, I know I didn't. I took the book along with the book I was looking at up to the register. Jermaine was gone for fifteen minutes. "Damn where is that boy?" I asked myself.

"I'm right here," Jermaine said appearing from behind me.

I jumped and said; "boy you scared me,"

He laughed. "I'm sorry. Where's Angel?"

"She looking at the books on the other side,"

Jermaine looked over the bookshelves then turned around and looked at me. "She ain't over there,"

"Well she around here somewhere," I placed the books on the counter and the lady behind the counter rung them up.

"Bitch what the fuck you mean 'she around here somewhere'? You better find my motha-fuckin sista."

Bitch, I know he did not just call me a bitch. You know what I'm just going to ignore the fact that he called me that; I was not trying to cause a scene in this mall. I knew something was strange about him and Angel, now that he mentioned it they do look alike, but why did he tell me that he didn't have any brothers or sisters. I gave the lady my money and waited for my change then took the bag and walked away. Jermaine walked up to me and grabbed my arm making me face him.

"Get the fuck off me;" I snatched my arm away from him.

"Where you goin?"

"Home!" I yelled at him.

"Find Angel!" He yelled back at me.

"Find her your got damn self,"

"Bit-"

"Boo!" Angel said cutting him off and jumping out from behind us. He looked down at Angel. "Girl, where were you?"

"In the store over there," she said pointing to every store on her left side.

"Don't you ever leave without telling anybody where you going."

"Okay."

"I'll see you when you get home Angel," I said.

"Why? Where you going?" Angel asked me.

"Home,"

"Ride with us. Where about to leave,"

"That's okay. I'm not going straight home anyway. Bye," she waved to me as I walked away.

Later that night when I got home Janette was sitting in my room. I sat my bags down on the floor beside my bed. "What you doing here?"

"Dang I can't come over here to see my best friend," Janette said.

"Again, what are you doing here?"

"Okay, come with me to see Brandon,"

"You mess with Brandon now?"

"Yeah, I been told you that. So are you gonna come with me?"

"Naw, I gotta go see Shawn in thirty minutes and I gotta meet James down in his office tonight,"

"Ne-Ne?"

"I know, I'm a break it off with James tonight,"

"What about Shawn?"

"What about him? I need some way to get my clothes and stuff,"

"How bout you get a job," Janette suggested as I went to my dresser and pulled out some under clothes.

"Girl please. I don't work,"

"You, you don't learn do you?"

"What?" I asked.

"I thought you stopped that stuff? I thought you were tryna get Jaquile back?"

"Don't worry about that, I'm gonna get my baby."

"Um, yeah okay." Janette said as got up and made her way to the door. "I'm bout to go get ready to see Brandon,"

"Aiight," she left and I went and took a quick shower, then got ready to head over Key' Shawn house.

When I arrived at Key' Shawn house I seen a cherry red Lexus parked outside of his house. I didn't really care if he had another girl in his house as cause it wasn't like he was my man he was just supplying me with my needs. I didn't bother to go up in the house; I just turned around and went right back home.

When I got home I seen Angel and one of her friends sitting on the couch watching an episode of Rug-rats. They looked like they were so into the show, it was one of my favorites too. Angelica was off-da-hook.

"Where James at?" I asked Angel.

"Uh, I think he's, um...I don't know," Angel said as she watched T.V.

"Where's Jermaine?"

"In his room, talking to some boys."

"Aiight," I said as I ran upstairs and ran past Jermaine's room with my ear's wide open.

"Man, I said I was gonna give you your money when I get it," I heard Jermaine semi yell at another person in the room. Me being the nosey person I am I stood by the door and listened.

"If you don't give me my money in the next two weeks that pretty little girl downstairs is going to be gone." The man said as he looked at me at the door, Jermaine followed his eyes and seen the man was staring at me. Jermaine slammed the door in my face and I jumped back, I put my ear up to the door and tried to see what else I could hear, but I couldn't hear anything else. I wondered whom that man was Jermaine was talking to. I wanted to know who it was so I sat on the steps until they came out. Moments later the man came out but not Jermaine, he was still sitting in there. When I got up to see what was wrong the man bumped into me knocking me down two steps.

"I mean damn, excuse you." I said to the man.

"Oh, my bad shawty," the man said as he starred at me up and down. "You cute as shit," I rolled my eyes and said, "Whateva." I continued up the steps and walked into Jermaine's room, while the man kept talking,

"When you finish messing with that punk, come to a REAL nigga," I shut Jermaine's door. He was sitting on his bed with his head in his hands. I was leaning on his door.

"How much you owe him?"

Jermaine looked up at me with tears in his eyes "None of your business. You are so fuckin nosey," he told me.

"I was just trying to help you out. I could get the money," I told him.

"Well guess what I don't need your help I could get the money on my own," he said with an attitude.

I glared at him. "You are so stubborn."

"And you're a hoe."

"Nigga, fuck you, you don't know shit about what I do."

"Bitch who don't know what the fuck you doing, you fucking the whole damn neighborhood."

"What the fuck ever."

"I'm not dumb like that nigga you got killed. I know when to draw the line with your ass." The next thing I knew I was running towards him with my fist flying, screaming cursing words at him. I couldn't control my anger, my built up frustration all came out. I was hitting him in his face trying my hardest to hurt him, but I knew that my punches didn't faze him. He tried to restrain me but I was too wild for him. In the mist of our tussling we knocked over his lamp. Mrs. Adams ran in the room with James right behind her. James pulled me away from Jermaine.

"Nigga, you betta watch your back." I screamed at Jermaine. He stood up and fixed his clothes.

"Bitch do what you do best and suck my mother-fuckin dick." He spat at me. Before I had a chance to say anything else to him James dragged me out of the room.

Later that night after thinking long and hard I told James that I couldn't keep seeing him, he kept asking me why and telling me that I didn't really want to stop seeing him, but when I stopped coming down to his office when he asked me to, he got the picture. I tried to stay clear of Jermaine. We never talked once we crossed paths, when we first fought we would give each other dirty looks, but a week after we stopped looking at each other. Jermaine came to me a month after that man paid him a visit.

"Alright, I need your help," Jermaine said to me.

"Need my help for what?" I asked.

"I need six-hundred," he told me.

"I'm not helping you with anything."

"Nevaeh, come on now. I'm not the begging nigga but if I have to I will. That nigga is talking about doing something to Angel."

"I'm a bitch remember. I'm not good for anything but sucking dick. Do you remember that stuff that you said to me?"

"Okay, I apologize. Now can you help me?" He begged.

"Again I'll tell you, no." He sucked his teeth and left out of my room.

A day after Jermaine came and asked for my help I thought long and hard about his situation. Despite the confrontation that we had I felt I needed to help him out. The look on his face looked so desperate. It was hard for me to think of a reason to ask Key' Shawn for some money but I came up with one. That night I found myself at Key' Shawn's house, lying on my back with my legs spread like an eagle. I exaggerated every moan as he pumped in and out of me. I felt grubby as his sweat dripped in between my titties. In my head I kept telling myself that I was doing it for something good so that I wouldn't feel as though I was letting myself down again.

I went home that night and threw the money on Jermaine's bed. He looked up at me.

"Aight, bet." He said. I stood at the end of his bed looking at him. "What?" he asked.

"That's all I get? What happened to a thank you?" a smirk came across his face. I just looked at him. In my head I kept thinking about how ungrateful he was and how I just degraded myself to keep him and his sister from being six feet under. I quickly snatched the money up and turned to walk out of the door. I heard him as he jumped up and ran in front of me before I had the chance to make it out of the door.

"Hol up, where you going?" he asked.

"Back to my room." I looked passed him out into the hallway. I just wanted to kick myself for thinking that we would become closer if I had helped him out with his situation.

"With the money though? I thought you was helping me out?"

"Can I get a damn thank you? I did all that shit to help you out; but I can't even get a damn thank you. So I'm taking this money and put it to use." I told him.

"Thank you." I made a face as if to say 'Yeah whateva' still looking out into the hallway. "Nevaeh, look at me." I turned to look at him. My eyes connected with his and from there I knew that he was the one for me. "Thank you."

Since that day I worked hard on trying to gain respect from Jermaine and to get my self-esteem back up. I no longer had the same attitude. Not caring what anyone else thought of me. I was now living for my son, trying to get him back in my life. I still thought about Quinton every night. I thought about how he could've lived a little longer if he didn't know me. On my road to overcoming the tribulations I found myself blaming my mother for my mistakes. If only she wasn't strung out she could've protected me from the demons that hid inside of me.

Months after Jermaine incident we began to talk more and became good friends. Well sex partners, we wouldn't sleep together every night because he didn't trust me that much but we did make it a routine to do it once or twice a week. Soon I had told him that I had completely cut all ties to Key' Shawn, a couple of weeks after telling him that we had made it official. School had started and I had talked Jermaine into going back to school; he was a grade higher than me, so that mean he was in the twelfth grade. I was sitting in my room when my cell phone rang. I looked at the caller ID then picked it up.

"Hello," I said into the receiver.

"Come over here," I heard Key' Shawn say into the phone.

I looked at the clock read 7:17p.m. "For what?"

"Cause I have to give you something."

"What is it?" I asked him frustrated because I was in the middle of doing a project that had to be turned in the next day.

"If you come over here you would see,"

"Bring it over here, because I'm in the middle of doing something."

"Trick bring your ass over here and come and get it. Don't try and act brand new cause you with that Nigga." He demanded.

I sucked my teeth, "Ain't no body acting brand new. I matured so I'm not getting into all of that anymore."

"Yeah alright; just come over here right quick. Just five minutes." I thought about it. Five minutes and that's it.

"I'll be over there." I told him.

"Aiight," Key' Shawn said then hung up the phone. I hung the phone up and grabbed my coat and headed out the house.

When I arrived at Key' Shawn's house I seen him, Brandon, and some other two boys who was dark chocolate one with dreads and one with a low cut fade. I walked towards the car as the cold November breeze hit up against my face.

"So wassup?" I said while looking at all of them. One of the unfamiliar boys was staring and walking in circles around me saying, "Damn dog, she thick as shit," he said then smacked my ass and the boys started laughing, I turned around to ready to slap him when Key'

Shawn grabbed my hand.

While laughing Key' Shawn said, "Lamar man, leave her alone, don't scare her off." He let go of me and got into his car followed by everyone else except me.

"Come on girl," Brandon yelled out the window.

"Naw, Key' Shawn said he had something for me. Now unless you gonna give me what you have for me then I'm gone." I said wrapping my arms around my body.

"It's over my boy house. That's where we headed to now. I'll drop you off at home as soon as you get it. Promise." I hesitated before I got in the car and sat between Lamar and the other unknown boy. I trusted Key Shawn and somewhat trusted Brandon; I mean he did go out with my best friend.

We were driving for what seemed like an hour when they pulled into this disserted area. Key' Shawn got out the car while the three of them stayed.

"Excuse me," I said as I tried to get out of the car but they had the door on child safety lock. "For real, let me out of this car." I told them.

"Why you trying to get out so fast, you don't want the present we have for you?" I can't remember everything that happened but I know they raped me; I kicked and screamed as hundreds of tears poured out of my brown eyes. My once caramel skin was now red. They roughly pulled down my pants as I fought to keep them up, one by one they forcefully went inside of me. I looked up and out the window and seen Key' Shawn staring down at me with a nervous look on his face, he was the last thing I seen before everything went blank.

When everything came back to me we were at my house and Key' Shawn was holding me up at my door. I kept hearing him whisper in my ear about how sorry he was, but I didn't want to hear that bullshit. My first reaction was to hit him, and that I did, I punched him right in his face then walked into the house slamming the door. I began to cry as I walked. Marissa, another one of the girls living in the house, startled me. She was coming from out of the kitchen, eating something. Her fat ass was always eating something, one day she is going to pop. I thought to myself.

"Are you okay?" She asked me with a mouth full of food. I nodded my head yes and continued to walk upstairs to my room. It was empty which meant Angel was either in Jermaine's room or over a friend house. I walked to my dresser and pulled out something that I hadn't used in a while. I walked into the bathroom as if I was a zombie, shut the door and locked it behind me. I turned on the shower and put it as hot as I can stand it. I sat on the toilet and took the blade and cut deep into my skin, I watched as the warm blood trickled down my arm. That was something I did to try and take the pain away. After I sat there for a while watching myself bleed, I took off all of my clothes and got into the shower trying to wash all the pain away. They made me feel so, so, so ugly and so dirty, I scrubbed my body until it felt like my skin was peeling off. When I got out the shower I walked into my room I put my under clothes on and an oversized t-shirt I got from Jermaine. I reached under my bed and pulled out my journal and began to write.

Beauty
I am Beauty
And oh yes Beauty is me
Now don't get me wrong my words don't speak conceit
I realize and I see
That my Beauty is more than skin deep.
I radiate Beauty
And Beauty shines upon me
I am Beauty and
Oh yes Beauty is me.
Now I repeat this because you may not understand
I am Beauty
Beauty is who I am
And not because I was told by some man
But because I was designed this way

By the Great I am
I was born in Beauty
I live in Beauty
I laugh in Beauty
And I will surely die in Beauty...
Miss Ameenah © 2004

That was the last thing I wrote before my door opened and Jermaine walked in and sat on my bed. I closed my book when he wrapped his arms around my waist and began kissing me on my neck.

He kissed me two more times before saying, "Where were you at?"

I responded by saying, "Out, where is Angel?"

He began kissing me again and reached under the cover that only hid my waist down and started rubbing on my inner thighs. I was sore from the previous terror.

"In my bed sleep," his hand got higher and higher as he intensely kissed my lips. I tried pushing his hand down away from my inner thigh and 'special area' but he brought it right back up. I was so sore, bruises hid on my thighs. I didn't want him the see the hideous marks on me.

"Come on girl," he said as he moved from my lips to my neck while getting on top of me.

I tried to pull away from him. "Stop," I told him. He didn't move, he continued to kiss and feel all over me. "I said STOP!" I pushed him off me, I pushed him real hard, and he fell on the floor.

"Damn, what the fuck!" Jermaine shouted.

"I told you to stop!" I shouted back.

"Any other time you'll be ready to do the shit,"

"This isn't any other time, so can you get out so I could go to sleep."

He looked me in my eyes and he semi yelled. "Why you actin like a fuckin bitch?" I didn't respond to him. His eyes moved from my eyes to my arm then back up to my eyes, he shook his head as he looked around the room. He looked over at the dresser and froze, I looked over at the dresser and seen my bloody towel and blade. I jumped up off my bed knocking my book on the floor and went over to my dresser picking up the towel and blade; Jermaine grabbed my right arm, the one that I had cut, making me flinch. He yanked the towel out of my hand making the blade fall to the floor. He held the towel up to my face and began yelling.

"What the fuck is this?" I didn't answer so he pointed to my arm, which was now bleeding. "What the fuck is this?"

"What the fuck do it look like?" I yelled back at him.

"What the hell is wrong with you? Cutting yourself...Are you crazy?"

"No, it's just something I do to feel better...to take the pain away...stress,"

I heard Mrs. Adams knocking on the door. "What are ya'll in there yelling about? Calm all that noise down, it's going on one o'clock in the morning and there is school tomorrow. Now go to sleep." I heard her walk away from the door.

"Do you always do this shit?" Jermaine asked.

"No. Just sometimes, I haven't done it in awhile though." I told him.

"What you gonna do when you cut yourself too deep and you can't stop the blood from running, huh? You need think man. You need to use your fuckin brain."

"Well if that do happen I guess I will just die. That's better than being here, right?"

Was it better than being here? Was it better than being in a world that had no heart? He let go of me and started pacing around the room, five minutes without either one of us saying anything, he then took a last look at me then he left out the room.

Chapter 10

I went to school the next day like I always did and tried to make it through all my classes without falling asleep. After my first period class I walked to my locker to change books, while I was there I was approached by Brandon and the dark skinned boy with the dreads. I felt a hand rub against my butt, my body became tense.

"Damn girl, when you gonna let me get up in that again?"

"Don't touch me." I said turning around facing them. I looked down breaking between the both of them. Not daring to look into the eyes of the guys who degraded me.

It was fourth period and it was lunch, I was on my way into the lunchroom when Janette came and stopped me.

"You can't go in there." She told me.

"Why not?" I asked her.

"Cause, you just can't,"

"Janette, unless you're gonna tell me why, move out of my way. I'm hungry and I'm not in the mood to be bothered with." I moved her out of my way and walked into the cafeteria. I walked passed by three tables before I noticed people whispering, looking and pointing at me.

"Aye ya'll there go that girl that sucked Lamont's dick." It hurt me when they said that, because they were accusing me of doing something that I didn't do and to someone that I didn't know; but I still held my head high. All of a sudden they just started singing that go-go song from UCB *(Uncalled for Band)*, a local band formed in Washington DC. "She's a hoe, she know she's a hoe. Fuck these niggas after every show." I didn't even get anything that day; I walked out the cafeteria. I stopped in my tracks when I seen Jermaine and some girl sitting on the railing outside. The girl was standing in between his legs while he sat on the rail, his hands were hanging over her shoulders and he was kissing on the nape of her neck. I wanted so badly to go out there and knock him and the girl up aside their heads, but my body wouldn't move. I couldn't even move from where I was standing to go home until he looked up at me, if looks could kill I would have been dead. His eyes gave off this vibe like he didn't care. That had broken my heart; the one person that I thought cared about me. When he looked up at me, I took a deep breath and rolled my eyes and walked away in the directions of my locker. I had went and got my stuff and took the side door and went home.

"Yo, let me talk to you for a minute." Jermaine came into my room and said to me. I looked up at him standing in my door way.

"What do you want?" I was still mad at him for the other day. His eyes darted over to where Angel was on the phone.

"In my room." I narrowed my eyes not wanting to go, but wanting to see what he had to say. Once we got into his room I went over to Quinton's desk that was still in the room and sat down. He had just gotten in the house so it was quite between the two of us while he got comfortable. The silence made me think about Quinton and the fun times that we use to have the times that he use to be my shoulder to cry on about my problems. The many times he went with me to go and visit Jaquile. If only he wasn't living with that incurable disease we could've had something; he knew things about me that Janette didn't even know.

"Aye youngin, we need to talk." He sat on the edge of his bed.

"So talk."

"First, my bad about disrespecting you and all with the cursing at you and everything; second, what's going on with you?"

"Ain't nothing going on with me, what's going on with you?"

"What do you mean what's going on with me?"

"You fucking other females?" anger could be heard in his voice.

"What? Don't bring that insecure shit up in here." He told me.

"Insecure? You the one kissing up on the bitch a couple days ago in front of the school, if anything that would probably give me reason to be insecure." He stood up off of his bed. I stood from the chair.

"Don't even bring that shit up when you still fucking Shawn." Just mentioning his name made my skin crawl. I began to yell at him.

"What the fuck do you want from me? Huh? I told you that I'm not fucking him anymore!" He tried to touch me, but I yanked away from him.

"Young calm your lil ass down."

"No, don't touch me! Fuck you and this mother-fuckin relationship!" I spat at him. I was so tired of trying. Trying to become someone better than how everyone expected me to be. "I'm not about to sit up here and try when your ass don't even trust me. If you think I'm fucking Shawn then I will go out and do it for real." The look in his eyes looked like they wanted to kill me. I began to walk out of the door when

I felt myself being yanked and thrown onto the wall making a loud bang.

"Fuck me Nevaeh!" One of his hands clinched my throat while the other one fondled with my belt. "Fuck me; yeah okay I'd fuck you aight!"

"Yeah, I knew that's what you were all about anyway. Just like the rest of this niggas out here. That's why I never took your ass serious." I mumbled. I felt myself being lifted up away from the wall, and then slammed back onto it, knocking a picture off the wall outside of the room. Someone began to bang on the door.

"Jay, what are you doing in there?" A soft voice said on the other end of the door.

"Get off of me." I demanded. My back was killing me but I refused to cry in his presence. He began to tighten his grip. "Get the fuck off of me Jermaine!" I felt my breaths getting shorter. We were starring each other in the eyes. I had a blank expression on my face while his had this cold stare, emotionless. I heard the door open and then heard someone yell for someone to come and help them. My vision began to go dark, but not before Jermaine came close to me and whisper into my ear.

"You fuck him, and I'm gonna kill your ass. Mark my words. You wanted this shit with me, now you got it." He said let me go, my limp body drop down to the floor gasping for air.

I stayed clear from Jermaine after that day he made attempts to try and come in my room to talk to me or cuddle with me but I would just go in Lisa's room and sleep in there. I knew that I was making him mad, but I didn't care. He threatened my life, and for what, because he had gotten caught up with messing with this chick? I knew that I wanted him, maybe started to catch feelings, but I couldn't allow myself to continue to be someone's doll on a string.

I remember Janette and I was sitting in the room watching television and Angel was in the room with Jermaine, when the phone rang. It only rung one time then stopped, so I picked it up.

"What you want?" I heard Jermaine say angrily. I was about to hang up when I heard Key' Shawn say, "Let me speak to your girl," So me being the nosey person that I am, I stayed on the phone. I waved my hand to try and get Janette's attention, she was just looking at T.V. so I picked up my brush that was lying on the bed and threw it at her. She looked at me with her face tied up, I smiled and mouthed the words 'turn the T.V. down,' and she did as I said.

"Nigga, I gave her everything she got. That cell phone you call her on, I gave her that. The money she gave you so you could pay youngin off, where do you think she got it from? Aye check her neck, did you see that necklace? That thing is wet. She wears it faithfully, everyday. All she gotta do is let me taste her sweet cat. Really, how you think she still be getting all that high shit? She ain't got no job," Key' Shawn said. I heard Jermaine clinch his teeth but said not a word. Key' Shawn continued to say, "Aye dog member what we did back in 9th grade. Now that bitch shit was nice and tight." Jermaine hung up the phone, so I hung up leaving Key' Shawn to listen to the dial tone. Janette looked at me trying to figure out what had gone down when Jermaine bust into the room. We both jumped.

"What the hell is your problem?" I shouted at him. He ignored me.

"Janette let me holla at Nevaeh right fast,"

"Aight, I'll call you tonight girl," Janette said.

"Aight," I told her. She grabbed her stuff and left out the room. Jermaine closed the door behind her and rested on the door. I sat on the bed feeling uncomfortable, afraid of what he might do. His temper was one that I didn't wasn't to experience again.

"Bit...I mean Nevaeh. I thought you said that shit was over between you and that nigga Key' Shawn," Jermaine yelled at me.

"What are you talkin about? That shit is over," I told him.

"Stop lying to me. I know you were sitting on the phone listening, I heard when you picked up the phone. And I know you heard that shit when he said what you are doing for money, clothes and shit. I knew you fuckin got around, but what the fuck! You prostituting, fuckin niggas for money? If you needed money or clothes that bad all you had to do was ask me, and you know that shit." He paused for a minute then continued, "If I knew you were going to go fuck him I wouldn't gotten you to help me out with what I needed help with." I stopped him before he had a chance to say something else.

"Oh that is bullshit Jermaine! You knew-you knew I was gonna go fuck him. Just admit it; you didn't care about me, or what I did to get your money." I watched him rub his hand over his face. He took two steps back and sighed. A look of uncertainty was written all over his face. He through his hands behind his head and closed his eyes. "All that shit I been hearing around school, that you let some nigga's run a train on you and you sucked one of them nigga's dick. I kissed you, on your mother-fuckin lips," he took a deep breath. I even saw some tears roll down his face. He didn't even bother to wipe them off, guess he wanted me to see his true feelings towards me. The way he carried himself made it seem like he had no emotion to show, like he didn't care about anyone but his family. I got up and stood in front of him touching his face trying to wipe his tears away. Some even came down my eyes. He opened his eyes and looked into mines. He started talking calmly to me.

"So that's why you was acting like that, that night you didn't want me to touch you. You were out fuckin Shawn or some other youngin."

With tears fluttering my throat I spoke. "No, no. Stop believing everything you hear, that's not what happened,"

"Well tell me what happened,"

"I can't. You won't understand,"

"Make me understand,"

"I can't," I took my hand off his face and turned my back to him.

"Damn, you don't know how much I love you; but I can't be with you anymore. I can't be with someone who I can't trust." I turned around surprised at what he said. Not the part where he said he can't be with me anymore or the fact that he couldn't trust me; but the part when he said that he loved me. I mean I was shocked when he said that other stuff but no boy has ever told me they loved me. His face was wet from all the tears that were coming out of his eyes. I was tearing him apart and didn't even know it. The thing about it I didn't feel the same way he did. Or did I? The phone rang, seconds later Angel came knocking on the door.

"What!" He screamed at her.

"Some boy name Key Shawn want to speak to Nevaeh," Angel said outside of the door.

"She's busy; tell him that she will call him back."

"Okay," Angel said. She walks away from the door. I finally speak.

"You told her that like I'm gonna call him back." He looked at me, starring me directly in the eyes. "So you're gonna leave me now?"

"It'll be best if we do break up. I am so tired of you fuckin all these different dudes. I can't be sharing my girl," Jermaine told me.

"You're not sharing me,"

"You can't even tell me what went down that night. Are you trying to think of a lie?"

"No, I'm not tryna lie!" I somewhat hollered at him.

He came back at me with the same tone. "Then tell me what the fuck happened!"

"They rapped me okay! Are you happy now that I told you! Brandon, Lamar and some other boy ran a train on me while Shawn just sat back and watched!" He didn't say anything, for a while, I called his name. "Jermaine?" he just turned and walked out the room. I walked out behind him I called his name again; he didn't answer me so when we got downstairs I grabbed his arm. "Jermaine I know you hear me talkin to you!" I screamed. He grabbed me then pushed me up on the wall.

"Why didn't you tell me that them niggas did that to you. Why do you have to keep a secret like that from me? Huh?" I didn't know he was that pissed off. He had a tight grip on my arm. I was scared because of the last time we had gotten into an argument.

"I promise that I won't keep another secret from you again. I promise," tears rolled out of my eyes. He looked at me then his eyes went from my eyes to my neck.

"Where did you get that necklace from?" his voice scared me. I hesitated before I said his name.

"Key'Shawn." He let me go, yanked the almost two hundred dollar necklace off of my neck, making my head jerk forward. I rubbed around my neck as I watched him grab his jacket off of the railing and left the house slamming the door behind him.

"Yeah Janette, he is so mad at me now." I said to Janette over the phone.

"Damn, I told you about this shit. Now you see what happened?" She told me.

"I know, but look; you know how females are seeing how that's what we are and you know how males are and you know sometimes they can make you melt and they can make you laugh and sometimes it's hard to resist. I'm just now figuring out my feeling for Jermaine and it scares me. I have never loved anyone before, I mean he's just like all the other boys I know or have had some type of encounter with, the only difference is that he cares about me. I just don't know what to do." I confessed to Janette. I don't even think she was listening to me. It was two in the morning and me knowing her, she went to sleep on me. There wasn't anyone here but me and the kids. The adults went to some painter's convention out of town and left Jermaine in charge since he was the oldest. After he stormed out of the house I slid down the wall crying. The slamming of the door startled some of the kids in the house causing them to come out of their room to see what was going on. I reassured them that I was okay. "I'll just call and tell you about it tomorrow Janette," she did say anything. I hung up.

Jermaine came home a few hours later. I was asleep on the couch; it was four in the morning. He came over and woke me up telling me to get up and go to bed; he had his hand on his side. He limped up the stairs; I waited five minutes before following him. I stood at his door and seen it cracked so I peeked through and seen him taking off his coat.

"Damn," I heard him say as he touched his left side. He lifted up his shirt and touched that same spot but this time when he removed his hand I seen that his side was badly bruised.

"Oh my God, Jermaine what happened?" I asked him as I walked over to him and kneeled down beside him. His side was bruised and swollen.

"Can you knock?" He asked me.

I ignored his question and continued talking, "Who did this to you?" I asked examining his side.

"Your boy,"

Still looking at his side, "Who's my boy?"

"Key' Shawn," I looked up at him as he looked down at me, looking at him for a second seemed like forever. I then turned my head and stood up.

"Key Shawn is not my boy," I told him.

"You fuck him like he is," he said coldly. It felt like a needle stuck me in the heart.

"I can't deal with you right now. I tell you what happened, I tell you that I'm not dealing with him anymore and you don't believe me. I don't know what to do anymore." Silence fell upon the room. "You need to go to the hospital." He just looked at me then limped over to his chair that sat in the corner of his room put his jacket back on. "Where are you going?" I asked concerned.

"Where do it look like I'm about to go?"

"Don't get smart Jermaine, I just asked you a fuckin question. You know what, just go, I don't even give a damn anymore." He stood up and once again left.

Since the night of the argument Jermaine and my relationship had been on and off for about four months, but all in all we been together for over a year. I watched how he would watch me while I was on the phone, listening to every word that came out of my mouth while trying not to be obvious. I never gained his full trust, and from the situation I don't think I ever will.

I was sitting in Angel and my room fixing my hair getting ready so Jermaine could take me out to some restaurant. It was our one year anniversary.

"Are you and my brother gonna get married?" Angel asked me. Shocked by her question I answered with, "I don't know. Do you want me to marry your brother?"

"If you want," I looked at her through the mirror and smiled. I made the final touches on my hair then stood up.

"How I look?" I asked Angel. I had on a tight fitting black lace dress, which showed nothing but skin and my hair in an up do.

"You look delicious," Jermaine said.

I turned and looked his way with a smile on my face, "I know, don't I" I said laughing while modeling off my dress.

Him and Angel laughed, "Your lil conceded ass. You ready?" He asked me.

"Yeah, let me just grab my purse." Jermaine gave Angel a kiss on the forehead and told her that we would be back and that he loved her then we left.

We went to this fancy restaurant out in Virginia, and then he took me to this club called Dreams in D.C. I don't know how he got us into the club and we were under age, but when we got in there we found ourselves a table and got a couple of drinks. After my second glass of Apple Martini I was ready to dance. We got on the dance floor and started dancing to Big Tymers "Gangsta Girl." I wasn't big on dancing so I didn't know what I was doing but I was doing something. After an hour of dancing to upbeat tempo's 112 "Cupid" came on. We began dancing slowly while his hands moved up and down my body.

"Let's go," he whispered in my ear. I didn't say anything I just grabbed his hand and lead him to the car. He took me to a motel and got a room. When we entered the room there was no words, second thoughts or looks. I just pushed Jermaine onto the bed and climbed on top of him kissing and creasing his neck with my lips, that night I wanted to be in control. While still kissing we pilled each other clothes off. I was ready and I knew Jermaine saw it in my eyes, I wanted him more and more by the second. We were kissing and the next thing I knew he flipped me over and his tongue began to explore my body. We made eye contact until he got down to my area, he began licking around my inner thigh then made his way to my click, and he began to tease me with his tongue. He finally gave in and let his tongue explore my insides as I leaned back and let my eyes explore the back of my head, enjoying what he was doing to me. Then he stopped. I looked down to see what was wrong, he was starring straight up at me, no talking, just looks.

"Watch," He told me in his sexiest voice. He continued. The whole time he was getting a taste of me we made eye contact. He didn't move in time so I came all in his mouth, he licked his lips and smiled at me.

"I'm a start calling you Cupcake," he told me.

"Why?" I asked him out of breath.

"Cause you taste so sweet,"

"Is that right?" I asked pulling him up on top of me.

"Yeah." He kissed me letting me taste all of my juices and it got more intense, we continued kissing as we got back to what we were doing. We were at it all night doing every position known.

Approximately three weeks after our anniversary I became sick as a dog. Throwing up everywhere, and a fever of 104 degrees; for three days I woke up in the middle of the night drenched in sweat. I was lying in my bed while Jermaine lay beside me wiping my head off with a cold cloth when I began coughing. Jermaine sat me up and I began to cough up blood. My body felt so limp. That's when he called the ambulance and I was rushed to the hospital; that night I found out I had leukemia. Jermaine and I were sitting in the hospital room talking about my situation. Ms. Adams had just left a couple minutes before with Mrs. Cummings tailing behind her.

"You know I got to move out by next week,"

"Yeah, I don't want you to leave me," I pouted my lips.

"Move in with me."

My eyes got big. "Move in with you?"

"Yeah, it'll be me, you and Angel,"

"And Angel?"

"Yeah Angel, what you thought I was gonna leave her in that house while I'm out with my own place."

"No baby, it's just that you know you won't be her legal guardian right. You gonna have to take this to court."

"Yeah, I know. I can do it. You gonna have my back right?"

I smiled up at him. "Of course."

"So you gonna come stay with me or what?" He asked me.

"Okay, I guess so." I told him a little hesitant.

When I got out of the hospital a month later my stuff was already gone. Jermaine had taken it to his apartment while I was still in the hospital. We moved to an apartment by Addison Road Metro station, just blocks away from the neighborhood where I grew up. It was small but big enough for the three of us. Angel and I were not legally supposed to be living with Jermaine because we were under age. We had worked out an agreement with Mrs. Adams as far as Angel living with us. She was ready for me to leave her house. Everything was going with the living situation until Jermaine received a letter in the mail stating that he's been charged with kidnapping of Angel, Jermaine was furious. That same day I found out that I was pregnant; I couldn't have another one, scared I couldn't take care of it like I couldn't take care of the other one. Scared they might take it away.

I remember Jermaine and I were sitting in our room arguing because I had just told him I was pregnant. Jermaine was sitting in our room arguing because I had just told him I was pregnant. Jermaine was sitting on the bed with his head in his hand.

"Are you gonna keep it?"

"Yeah, I have no other choice." I told him.

"Get an abortion," he said as he raised his voice.

I yelled at him, "I'm not getting an abortion!" he howled back at me,

"Well do something, shit! I'm not ready for a damn child."

"How the fuck you think I feel? I'm not even twenty and I'm about to bring another child into this fucked up world." I saw Jermaines' head shoot up.

"Another child?"

"I don't wanna talk about it." I told him as tears formed in my eyes. He stood up and began pacing around the room yelling.

"No, we gonna talk about this right now! Another child, another child! I don't even remember the first one!" with tears streaming out of my eyes I talked in a soft tone. "I have a three year old son."

"Who's the father? Is it Key'Shawn's?" He asked me bringing his voice back down to a mellow tone.

"No!" I yelled at him.

"Well who? I mean come on now what happened to no more secrets being kept between us?" Yelling in a stern voice I told him,

"I said I don't want to talk about the shit right now!" my eyes red and my head was thumping from all the screaming we were doing.

"I don't care what you want, you got kids and ain't telling me shit. I'm not bout to sit and raise another man's child!" he screamed.

"Ain't nobody asked you to do all of that. I can take care of my own."

"Then where the fuck is he then?" I grew silent. "huh?"

"He's in a foster home." I told him, ashamed. He did a sarcastic laugh.

"So who's this child's father Nevaeh?" My face was drenched with tears. He looked at me. I saw disappointment written on his face. He grabbed his jacket and left the room slamming the door behind. I heard Angel ask if she could go to one of her little friend's house, I heard him to tell her to ask me, and then the door opened then slammed shut. He was always leaving every time something jumped off. Angel came running into the room.

"I'm going over Nikki's house." I just nodded my head and she left out the room.

Jermaine came home around one something in the morning. I guess he thought I was asleep, but I was wide awake. He took off his clothes and climbed under the streets, turning his back towards mine; I turned towards his back and began whispering in his ear.

"I'm sorry I didn't tell you before, I was um…embarrassed."

"Embarrassed about what?" I grew silent. He sucked his teeth. "If you gonna keep getting quiet don't talk about it."

"Because I couldn't take care of him," he turned and faced me.

"What happened to him?"

"Social services took him away. I wasn't able to take care of him, but I still go to see him every chance I get. He knows who his mama is; I got one more year then I could get my baby back." I told him.

"How old is he?"

"He will be turning four in July." He looked up then back into my eyes.

"Thirteen, you were only thirteen when you had that baby?" tears began to come out of my eyes.

"Yes, I didn't know what to do when I found out I was pregnant." I coughed.

"Who's the father?" he asked me.

"I, I don't know." See the thing was I was sleeping with so many men that I don't know whom I got pregnant by; I was out sleeping with different men every night for money or clothes.

"Aw shit, my chest hurt," I said while holding my chest.

"You aight?" Jermaine asked me sounding concerned.

"Uh yeah, yeah I'm okay. Can we talk about this tomorrow?" I said lying.

"You sure you okay? Did you take your pills today?"

"Yeah," I lied.

“Don’t sit and lie to me.”

“I’m not.” He didn’t say anything else; he just looked at me then wrapped his arms around my waist and fell asleep.

Chapter 12

Some weeks later I found myself back in the hospital with Jermaine by side. I was getting worst and worst by the second; my hair was shedding like a dog I had gotten so pale. A doctor came in with a clip board in his hand; Jermaine was sitting with his chair beside me talking when the doctor called his name. Jermaine got up and they walked out the room; minutes later Jermaine came back in and sat in his seat and started shaking his head.

"What? What's wrong?" I asked him. He looked at me then said,

"Why you keep lying to me?"

"What are you talking about?" I asked again clueless.

"Why you not taking your pills, are you trying to kill yourself and the baby?" he asked me. He finally accepted that I had a son and that I was pregnant. "Tell me why you not taking your pills. Do you want this child or not?"

"Yes," I looked down at my hands as I played with them.

"Then why you not doing what the doctor asked of you?"

"-because, it's not doing anything but making me even sicker then I was before. Look at me, my hair falling all out." I told him.

"Look at you. Why you always thinking about yourself? You do have someone else growing inside of you. You ain't doing nothing but being selfish; and you wonder why they took your son away from you. Why are you always thinking about yourself?" I didn't know what to say, to him I was being selfish; but to me I was doing me and the baby a favor. That medicine wasn't doing anything but hurting us. It was quiet between the both of us as the doctor walked back into the room. I looked up at him.

"We're gonna have to keep you over night. Then we will need you back in here for some chemo-therapy." I took a deep breath.

"Is it possible that I can stop taking the meds while I'm pregnant and pick it back up after the baby is born?" I asked the doctor.

"We recommend that you take the meds now, so that nothing will complicate the pregnancy. Okay?" I nodded my head. I looked at Jermaine sitting beside the bed with his head down. I rubbed the top of his head.

"So I'll give you two sometime to talk, and I'll be back." With that said the doctor left the room.

"What's wrong Jermaine?"

"I love your ass, but you do stupid shit, you know that. For this relationship to work you have to start thinking about other people." I nodded my head. "Give me a kiss before I leave. You know I gotta go to court tomorrow morning." He leaned down and peaks my lips.

"Good luck baby. Come see me when you get out." I told him. With that he left. I stayed in and out of the hospital for about a month, and then I was released to go home with Jermaine watching over me making sure I took my medicine. Even though I was sick and pregnant didn't stop me from continuing school.

I sat in the third row beside some unknown boys listening to the old white man speak. I sat there for about two hours listening to people talk and sing until Ms. Wilson, the principle, got on stage. She began talking for a nit then announced valedictorian; she talked for five minutes before getting off of the stage. Ms. Wilson got back on stage and began calling names. Tamika Sayles, Tarell Sayles, D'Angelo Simpson, she called, still not mine. I was in a daze when the boy beside me nudged me in my side.

"Nevaeh Smith," Ms. Wilson said smiling. I smiled to myself and began walking towards her. Before walking on stage I fixed my white gown, belly popping out my gown, not ashamed at all. Most of my hair fell out so I just got a short hairstyle like Halley Berry use to wear her hair. As I accepted my diploma I looked out into the audience, I seen

Angel, Jermaine, and Ms. Cummings smiling at me taking pictures. I got off stage and went back to my seat letting the program continue.

After the ceremony Angel and Jermaine took me out to eat at Olive Garden. I ordered me some spaghetti and garlic bread; boy was it good.

"So Angel, how do you feel about becoming an auntie?" I asked her.

"Are you serious, are you even sure that baby is Jermaine's? Angel asked me. I looked down at my stomach, and then looked at Jermaine; he was sipping on his coke trying not to look at me. Once he looked at me I stared straight into his eyes as I spoke.

"Yes I'm sure this baby is his," I looked back at Angel. "Why would you ask me something like that?"

"Well because Jermaine said-"she started to say before Jermaine cut her off.

"So baby, have you decided on what you wanted to do about college yet?" Jermaine asked me.

"What did Jermaine say Angel?" I asked Angel completely ignoring Jermaine.

"Well, he said, that the baby might be-"Jermaine cut her off again.

"Angel, shut up," Jermaine told her.

"Why she gotta shut up?"

"Cause I told her to," Jermaine said to me. I sucked my teeth then starred down at my plat; I was no longer hungry.

"I'm ready to go." Jermaine looked up at me from his bowl of Chicken Alfreado.

"What the fuck is wrong with you?"

"You've officially pissed me the fuck off, and I want to go home now!" I stood up and threw my napkin on the table. When I turned around I saw nearby tables watching us. I didn't care, I wasn't gonna keep having him talking about me behind my back, thinking that I wasn't going to eventually find out. I stood outside of the car as I watched him and Angel walk out of the restaurant, talking to each other only loud enough for the two of them to hear. As soon as he unlocked the door I hopped into the back seat.

"Get your ass in the front seat." He told me. I leaned on the door by the passenger side.

"Leave me alone Jermaine."

"Nevaeh, you pissing me off; don't make me have to drag you up to the front seat." I kept quiet. "What the fuck is wrong with you huh?"

"Jermaine, please; we'll talk about this when we get home." I told him. He looked at me one more time then got into the driver's seat. Once angel climbed into the car he pulled off and we headed home in complete silence.

*

"What is it that you're saying about me? You can tell me. The baby might be what? You think the baby isn't yours? You still think I'm fuckin somebody else?" I yelled at him. "When I tell you that I haven't done anything with anybody else other than you since that night I got raped, I mean it. If you can't trust me, tell me now and I would leave you alone. I would pack all of my shit and leave. I will take care of my child my got damn self." He didn't say anything; he just looked as if he was in deep thought. I was just tired. Tired of living this life, tired of being judged, tired of having no one to run to when things go wrong, tired of being me, and tired of living in this world.

"Aight Nevaeh," was all he said. I rolled my eyes and went into our bedroom. I stayed in the room for awhile crying and thinking about the emotional stress I was going through. It was time for Jermaine to decide what he wanted. I wobbled into the living room where he was. I sat on the other couch across from him. Without looking away from the television he spoke.

"What?" I took a deep breath.

"Look at me." I demanded his attention. He looked at me. "I love you okay. I want to be with you. You told me that you were okay with my son and the child that is growing inside of me. If you had doubts about this child you come to me. Not your sister and not your friends.

ME." He didn't respond to what I had said out of my mouth, he just turned his attention back to the TV.

As time passed Jermaine and I grew further and further apart, there were so many nights when I would go to sleep without him next to me and then wake up without him holding me. Four months had gone by and I didn't know the status of the court case with him and Angel. By the fourth month mark he stopped coming home all together. It hurt me to know that I ran someone away. I tried showing up at his job, but every time I went up there his boss would tell me that he was out on a project. The many nights I cried wanting to be this perfect girl only showed me that I wasn't worth loving. Every doctor's appointment I had he wasn't there, the hand that was supposed to be held when I had to stay overnight at the hospital was always cold.

Nights when I couldn't sleep because he was constantly on my mind I would call Ms. Cummings; she was the only one I learned I could trust. The only one that I knew would have my back no matter what there were many nights when I sat on the phone crying to her about my problems with Jermaine.

No matter how much Ms. Cummings trued to make me think positive I just kept thinking about what everyone been telling me since I was old enough to know better. *'You're always thinking about yourself.' 'You're so damn selfish.'* It kept playing in my head as I walked into my bedroom and opened my top dresser draw. The silver blade shone underneath the moon light. He wasn't there for me to talk to about my problems like he always said he would me. I sat on the edge of my bed and rolled up my sleeve exposing my forearm. I closed my eyes as the blade pierced deep into my skin. Tears managed to squeeze out of my tightly sealed eyes. I sat and thought of how I tried to take two steps forward but was really taking three steps back.

A month before my due date I was sitting in the house watching Sex in the City still waiting for Jermaine to come home. I was all into it when somebody jumped on the bed beside me.

"Ma, can I sleep in here with you?" my son said getting under the covers. Jaquile Jaharvey Smith, that's his name. I got him back the day after my birthday. Jermaine came back home for awhile once Jaquile moved in, I guess to get the feel of having a child around. I never asked him where he had been all that time, I was just glad that he had come home. My happiness was soon laid to rest once he started hanging out all hours of the night again. Jaquile had grown attached to Jermaine, his eyes would light up whenever Jermaine would walk in the room; but it was like he was pushing my child away. I remember this one day when Jaquile called him daddy, Jermaine just stared at him then left out of the room. That's when he started hanging out all hours of the night and Angel would spend most of her time at her little friend's house. They made me feel as though they didn't want me or my son around them, if it was like that all they had to do was tell me and I would have found someplace else to stay. It was like Jaquile and I were the only ones living there because no one was ever home but us.

"Boy why you ain't sleep?" I asked Jaquile.

"Because I can't sleep so I came in here with you. Where's Jermaine?"

"He's working late. Go to sleep." Jaquile turned over and within seconds he was sleep. I watched a little bit of the one o'clock episode of Comic View before falling asleep myself.

'Three more weeks and I could finally get this girl out of me.' I said as I rubbed my belly. Life was going good since I had found myself a little job working as a receptionist at this temp agency. I could no longer depend on Jermaine; it was time for me to do what was right for me and my kids. I went to multiple job interviews before I found the receptionist job I had. It was my very first job and I was nervous but at the same time excited. I made sure I was there on time every day. I woke up three hours early because I had to drop Jaquile off at the day

care center that was on the opposite side of my job. Every day I would come home exhausted but I had to do what I had to do.

It was a Saturday and I was home relaxing after a long week of work. I was the only one home; Jaquile was down stairs at one of his new playmates house, and Jermaine and Angel still didn't bother to show their faces. I was lying down in my bed watching 'The Parkers' when I got a call from this girl name Taneesha.

"Hello?" I said into the phone.

"Yeah is this Nevaeh?"

"Yeah, who is this?"

"My name is Taneesha, and I'm just calling to let you know that Jermaine has been living with me for the past three months." She told me.

"Oh really?"

"Yes, he says-"I cut her off.

"So why are you calling me telling me that he's been staying with you? Are you trying to start something, cause I really can care less." I told her. I was lying; my heart was shattering as we spoke. I knew he was with another female I just didn't want to believe it.

"No, I just wanted to let you know where your man was, and who he was coming home to every night." Taneesha told me.

"If he's coming home to you every night wouldn't you think that he's not with me anymore and he's your man now?" I didn't wait for her to respond. "I can care less where he's resting his head right now, but thank you anyway for letting me know." With that said I hung up the phone I couldn't do anything but cry. Crying because my heart hurt, crying because he didn't want me anymore, and crying because he was doing the same thing I did to him.

I cleaned my face up and got out of bed. I went into the bathroom and washed up and put something comfortable on. I wasn't going to keep on stressing over him. If he didn't want me anymore I was going to leave. I went into our bedroom and packed some of me and Jaquile's things and placed them by the door. I then began cleaning up all the mess Jaquile made earlier. After I finished cleaning up all his mess I went back into the room I once shared with Jermaine and got ready to wash clothes. I was going through a pair of Jermaine's jeans when I found a yellow sheet of paper that had a phone number on it, and above it said, 'Key'Shawn's Cell.' Now I'm thinking that it wouldn't hurt to call and see what he's been up to. I thought about everything he has put me through, and then sat it on the nightstand. I put a load in the washer, then grabbed the phone and number and sat on the bed.

"Yo, who's dis?" I heard Key'Shawn ask.

"Key'Shawn?" I asked.

"Yeah, who's this?"

"Nevaeh,"

"Oh what! What's going on with you?" Key'Shawn asked me shocked.

"Nothin, tryna live,"

"True, so I hear you got one in the oven,"

"Yeah, I can't wait until she comes out. She is driving me crazy." I paused wondering in the back of my mind how he knew Jermaine. So I asked him. "I thought you and Jermaine weren't cool like that?" I asked out of curiosity.

"We weren't, but we got through it. That's how family is; we fight but no matter what he's still my cousin."

"Cousin?" I had to make sure I was hearing clearly.

"Yeah, he ain't tell you?"

'Oh my God, They're cousins and I fucked them both.' "No he didn't tell me that."

"Oh well, yeah that's my cousin."

"Well why ya'll not close or whateva?"

"Aight well it's like this-" we talked for over an hour. He told me how when they were younger they were like white on rice until they got into middle school and started hanging around this certain group of people. For them to be accepted but this group of delinquents they had to gang rape this girl. He explained how Jermaine didn't want to, but he looked up to Key'Shawn and when Key'Shawn talked to him about it he agreed to. After the incident Jermaine didn't look at him the same. There was so much hostility between the two of them. After him telling me that I had gotten a cold chill. I guess that was why he had gotten so angry when I told him that I was raped.

"So why now ya'll started talking?" I asked.

"Because he called me one night threatens to kill my ass; I'm like dude what are you talking about? He talking about I fathered your child. I didn't even know you had a shawty." He told me. "So after we got that shit cleared and out the way he called me about three weeks later asking me what he should do about you being pregnant." I nodded my head as if he could see me.

"Have you talked to Janette?" he asked me changing the subject.

"No, the last time I talked to her was about a year ago.

"Damn, so you don't know that she's about to get married."

"Married to who?"

"Who do you think?" he asked me daring not to say his name.

"Um, well I'm happy for her." I grew quiet on the phone. I could hear him on the other end of the phone yelling at someone. I guess they were across the street. "Why did you take me so that those dudes can rape me?"

"What?" he asked me. I knew he heard me clearly, but I repeated myself anyway. "I donno; why did you use me?"

"Key'Shawn you knew what it was before we even started messing around on a regular basis."

"Yeah I did, but we can't change the past can we?" I got quiet. He sighed. "Why did you call me Nevaeh?"

"I just wanted to see how you were doing, and I wanted to see if you talked to Jermaine."

"Yeah I talked to him."

"So he's staying with another bitch huh?"

"How you know?"

"Because she called me and told me that that's where he now rests his head. I don't care though as long as he's paying the bills here I'm okay." He chuckled.

“Still money hungry,” I rolled my eyes. “But you still care, if you didn’t you wouldn’t be wondering if I talked to him. I got quiet again. I heard the front door slam shut.

“Jaquile don’t slam that door!” I yelled. “Are you ready to eat?” I didn’t get an answer but I felt a presence in the room as I looked in the doorway there stood Jermaine. I didn’t know what to do or say, all these emotions just swarmed together. I guess I was quiet for too long because Key’Shawn started yetting my name into the phone.

“Oh, my bad Shawn, let me call you back.” I hung up on him.

“So you and that nigga back at it again?” Jermaine asked me placing a box on the bed beside me. With an attitude I answered.

“Does it look like I’m with him?”

“Don’t answer me with a question,”

“Don’t ask me any fuckin questions,”

“Why you trippin, what’s wrong with you?”

“I’m trippin because some bitch called here telling me shit about ya’ll fuckin, and you gonna kick me out and take custody of my baby when I have it. The baby that you don’t even think is yours. Where have you been for the last two months?”

“I’ve been out tryna clear my head,” he told me.

“Clear your head where?” I asked.

“Why? I come home to see how you doing and you giving me shit.”

“Jay I’m just gonna go and stay somewhere else.” I went and picked up the bag and tried to walk out the door but Jermaine stopped me.

“Wassup with you, where you going?”

“Move Jay, I’m not in the mood,”

“No sit down so I could talk to you,”

“Didn’t I just tell you I wasn’t in the mood for your bull shit,” he snatched the bag out my hand. I mugged him and sat on the bed.

“Now open that box I gave you.” I turned around and grabbed the black box that looked like it held a rind inside, and turned back around. I opened the box only to find a piece of paper in it.

“Read it,” Jermaine said. I looked at him then looked at the paper, it read:

'As I stare into the bottomless pit, I sink into your eyes and fell to your heart. I hold your soft hands, breath in your sweet perfume and whisper I love you in your ear. You then give me a breeze-like kiss on my check. As I wrap your arms around my neck and I kiss your soft pink lips I pull you closer to me. My heart is beating hard and fast and I want to hear it. I tell you love begins with a smile, grows with a kiss and ends with a teardrop. Then I give you another kiss on the lips and I tell you "If there ever comes a day when we can't be together, keep me in your heart because you will always be in mine." You look at me then smile and nodded your head yes. As I held you tightly in my arms and a cover is wrapped around us. I give you soft kisses on your neck and I wish this moment would never end. You don't say anything but you smiled and I knew you feel the same way. I then start nibbling on your ear and move my hands up and down your soft smooth body. You get goose bumps and I whisper I love you. You say okay like you don't believe me. I say that there are a lot of ways to say I love you, but there is only one way to mean it. I know that it is hard to believe a thief. You say how are you a thief and I say because I took your virginity and I stole your heart. You look back at me with a smirk on your face and I look into your deep brown eyes and I say I would never rob you of your trust so you can believe me when I say it."

I was crying and didn't even know it. Jermaine was kneeled down right in front of me and wiped my tears away.

"I know I'm not your first, but I was your first love and I was your first in making love and hopefully I would be your last. So-"he pulled out a ring out his pocket and took my hand. "I know I haven't been there for you when you needed me most but I promise to be there for you from this day forward. Do," he took a deep breath then exhaled, "would you marry me? Please?" I didn't know what to say, I looked into his hazel eyes, which showed me love, care and affection. I seen the man I fell in love with. I couldn't marry him, not right now anyway. I gave him an answer that I knew would hurt him.

"No," I blurted out.

"No?" he asked hurtfully on the verge of tears.

"I meant to say I have to think..." I grabbed my stomach and it felt like I was pissing on myself. I mouthed, 'Oh my God," Jermaine looked at me with a puzzled look on his face.

"What's wrong with you?" Jermaine questioned me.

"It's time," I said taking deep breaths. He hopped up off of the floor and helped me up. I cried out in pain as I felt a contraction. I cursed obscenities at him as we made our way to the car. "Please call Mrs. Mayo and let her know that I went into labor. Jaquile is down there." He nodded his head and speed down the road.

Chapter 13

Ten hours of labor. I was in so much pain but it was worth it. I had a baby girl. I named her Jade Brianna Wilson. She came out looking just like Jermaine but light like me. She had big fat cheeks, red skin tone, a little button nose, and those big hazel eyes. There was no denying his child.

"Do you still think she belongs to someone else?" I asked Jermaine. He looked at me,

"Naw, I know she's mine." Jermaine was sitting in a chair by the bed holding Jade. Someone knocked on the door then walked in. it was Angel and Jaquile. Angel went over to Jermaine while Jaquile came over to me.

"She looks just like you Jay," Angel said. I don't think she like me anymore. I mean she used to want to be around me all the time, now that she's fourteen, she wants as little to do with me as possible.

"She looks like you too Angel," I told her. She just smiled at me.

"I'm sleepy," I told them fake yarning. Jermaine looked at me then said,

"Why don't ya'll wait outside of the door while I talk to Ne-Ne right fast, and then we could go home." They left out of the room and shut the door behind them.

"Why are you letting her get to you?" Jermaine asked me still holding Jade.

"I'm not," I told him. "Just because I jst had the baby doesn't mean I'm over what happened the past four months. I'm moving out when I'm released. You can come and see Jade whenever you want to." He laughed to himself.

"No you're not," he told me.

"Jermaine, when I get out of here can you have all my stuff packed?" I asked of him.

"Where you gonna go?"

"I don't know but I will find a place. I do have a job." I informed him.

"A job, when did you get that?" he asked surprised.

"While you were lying with some other chick."

"Don't do this Nevaeh,"

"Then leave," he starred at me.

"I'm gonna talk to Angel," he handed Jade to me. "I'll be back later," he leaned down and tried to give me a kiss, but I turned my head making him catch my cheek.

"Yeah aight," he left. I had to stay in the hospital a little while longer to get some test ran. Jermaine want to take the baby home a couple of days after she was born but I told him no. my baby was to stay with me until I went home. Jermaine kept Jaquile while I was in the hospital and he loved that, that's what my baby needed, a male figure in his life. While I was sitting in the hospital room late at night I did a lot of growing up and maturing as far as my living situation and I realized that I had no right to blow up on Jermaine when I did far more worst things to him when we begun talking.

Everyone on the staff was wonderful; they took real good care of me. There was one in particular, Mrs. Lawson; she catered to my every need, made me feel like I was a queen. When I looked into her eyes I seen happiness but yet pain. She reminded me so much of my mama when I looked at her. I took notice in the way that she was looking at me, and in the back of my mind I was hoping that she wasn't gay or anything. One night I was sitting in the room starring at the blank walls. I heard the door open then close; I looked towards the door and seen Mrs. Lawson come in and walk towards me.

"You're up, I thought you would be sleep." Mrs. Lawson said. Playing with my fingers I said,

"Naw, I can't wait to go home tomorrow,"

"I know you can't being cooped up in this hospital for a week or more is not where it's at." She said to me. "Your parents didn't come up here to visit you while you were here, I know you miss them." I shrugged my shoulders.

"I don't have any of those." I told her.

"Any siblings?" she questioned. I shook my head.

"I did but not anymore,"

"You know what happened to her?" I shook my head again. "What if I was to have told you that I knew where your sister was?" I looked at her. I never told her that the sibling that I did have was a sister. I guess she seen the questioning look that I had on my face because the next thing I knew, she jumped on me and embraced me in a hug.

"GOD! I missed you so much. Look at you, you grown up to be so beautiful," she pulled back and looked at me. I looked at her like she was crazy. She noticed the way I looked. "You don't remember me, it's me, Heaven!"

"Stop playin with me," I told her.

"I'm not playing." I just looked at her with a stuck face. All these years of not having my sister and now I have her. The things I went through and didn't have anyone to talk to about them with, now she's here. She was so pretty, you could say that her and my mom was a splitting image except she had a moa right above her lip, on the left side of her face. My face was wet with tears. I pulled her back into a hug and cried more. Tears fluttering my throat I spoke,

"I have so much to tell you."

We talked that whole night about our past, and everything we missed out on.

"So do I have any nieces or nephews?" I asked now excited.

"We're working on it." She said.

"We?" I questioned.

"Yes we, my husband and I." I nodded my head. "I've been married for about three years now. That's why my last name is not the same anymore."

"Oh okay, I'm so proud of you."

"So my nephew, what's he like?" she asked.

"He's a little boy, you know they're bad, but he will drop everything to help his mommy in a heart beat." I told her. "That's my little Romeo." She smiled.

"I want to meet him."

"You will," I told her. We talked until we fell asleep around five o'clock in the morning. Jermaine came and picked me up around ten o'clock that morning. I asked Heaven for some advice about getting married to Jermaine, the only thing she told me was,

"Since I don't know him all I could say is follow your heart." Like that was some help. We exchanged numbers and addresses.

For over the past month Heaven and I have become extremely close. I had began to talk back with Janette, her relationship with Brandon was holding strong, they planned to get married that December; she made me her maid of honor. Angel's attitude towards me has gotten a little better. She still didn't come and talk to me as much as she use to but things were getting better.

One day in October I was on the phone with Heaven talking about our day when out of nowhere she tells me how I needed to go and see our mother.

"No, I am not going to see that woman," I told her.

"Why not?" she asked.

"Because I can't forgive her for what she let them men do to me. Is she still taking her *'medicine'*?" I asked being sarcastic.

"Nevaeh, how long ago was that? It's time for you to forgive and forget."

"That's easy for you to say, you didn't have to go through what I went through," I told her.

"And why didn't I? You act like you were the only one hurt as a child, I was too; but I grew up." *'That's because you were throwing yourself at those men'* "You can't keep dwelling on the past." She told me. I nodded my head like she could see what I was doing.

"Just think about it. You got the address if you wanna go." I got quiet on the phone. "How about you come to church with me Sunday?" she suggested.

"Heaven you know I don't do that." I told her.

"You need to. You need to think him for bringing you threw all that mess he's brought you through. I can't pressure you to accept Jesus Christ as your savor, but just know that faith in God cleans us from sin. Just think about it okay. I'll holla at you later, I gotta go."

"Okay, just call me when you get back." She agreed and then hung up. After I hung up the phone I sat and thought about what she had just said. It would be nice to get a couple things off of my chest. From what Heaven had told me she had finally put that needle to rest. It would be nice to feel the warmth of my mother after all these years, let her know that I was doing well. Maybe meet her grandchildren one day.

"Let me make a doctor's appointment while Jade is sleep" I said to myself. I grabbed the phone getting ready to dial the doctor's office when the phone rang.

"Hello?" I asked.

"Stay the fuck away from Jermaine." The girl said on the other end. I took the phone away from my ear and looked at it. *'These bitches getting real bold.'*

"Who the hell is this?" I said.

"Almost a month ago I called. Jermaine said you won't leave him alone. So I advise you to leave him alone. " As she told me that Jermaine walked into the room.

"Baby, if you want him you can have him. I really don't care." I hung up on her. I watched Jermaine as he walked to the dresser and took his wallet and keys out his pocket and placed it in the dresser. He turned around and seen me starring at him.

"What?" he asked me.

"You need to tell your bitch to stop calling here," I told him.

"What bitch, who you talking about?"

"Natasha, TaNeesha, whateva her name is." When I said her name his eyes widened and he quickly turned his head away from me. "If you gonna leave me do it now. Tell me so I could get my shit and go. Like I told you before don't go running your mouth about me like I'm not going to find out. I am in this house everyday when I come home from work, so if you have a problem with me you know where to find me." I continued to say. I was serious, dead serious. Taking his shirt off he said,

"Neavaeh ain't nobody leaving your ass so stop trippin." I rolled my eyes at him and grabbed my keys and jacket.

"Where are my kids?" I asked him.

"Why, where you going?"

"Out of this house," I went into the closet and grabbed one of my duffel bags out and walked over to the dresser and began filling it up with some of my clothes and walked out of the room. I walked into Jade's room and put some of her things in there as well, I then walked into Jaquile's and seen him in there watching television.

"Jaquile put your coat and shoes on," I told him before going to his dresser and putting something in there for him as well. As he was putting his shoes on I was leaving out the room and going back into Jade's room. I dressed Jade and walked back into my room where I found Jermaine laying on the bed watching television. I walked over to my side of the bed and got a pieve of paper off of the nightstand. Jaquile came in and stood in the door way.

"Ma, I'm ready," Jaquile said.

"Alright, tell your father bye so we could go,"

"Where ya'll going?" Jermaine asked while doing the handshake he taught Jaquile to do awhile ago.

"Where not staying here with you anymore." I said shifting Jade from one arm to another. Jermaine shot up.

"What you mean you can't stay here," I walked out the room with Jermaine following right behind me into the front of the apartment and into the living room where Angel was lying on the couch.

"Like I said Jermaine, I'm not with this girl keep callin this house. Now if you care about this relationship you would tell her to stop callin here. But for now me and my kids are staying somewhere else." I handed Jaquile Jade's diaper bag.

"Those kids are just as much mine as they are yours!" he raised his voice. Jermaine when I referred to the kids as "*My* kids." Without thinking I said the first thing that came to mind.

"No, that's where you're wrong! Jaquile is nowhere near being your child, so get the shit right. Like I said before me and my kids are staying somewhere else until your bitch stop calling my house." I said placing Jade in her swing chair.

"No!" Jermaine yelled at me. "That's where you're wrong. This is my got damn house, I pay the bills, and I buy the food. I brought everything from the clothes you got on your back to shit *your* son plays with. I'm getting tired of you complaining when all you do is sit around the house and do shit."

"I don't do shit! I took care of this house when your ass was out for three months straight fucking God knows how many bitched. I got me a fuckin job Jermaine. I'm taking care of my own now." I was furious.

"You want to bring up me fucking other bitches. Yeah I was out fucking other females so what; but I brought my ass back home to you. So what the fuck is you getting mad for? We not going to get into all the niggas that you let up in you. Don't do it Mariah!" he yelled calling me by my middle name. "Angel take the kids in the room." He demanded. Angel hopped off of the couch and grabbed Jade and motioned for Jaquile to follow her. I shook my head.

"No, my kids are coming with me!" Angel stopped in her tracks and looked at the both of us not knowing which one to obey. Jermaine shifted his eyes from me to Angel.

"Do as I said and take the kids in the room, now!" this time Angel moved faster than what she did before and I kept quiet. Once she closed the bedroom door all hell broke loose.

"I'm not the same lil ass girl from back in that home. You keep throwing the shit I did in the past back in my face. You act like your shit don't stink, like you never did anything wrong in your life. I know all about you rapping some little girl when you were younger so don't throw shit in my face!" I looked at him and seen hurt and anger burning deep within his soul, the shit I said to him hurt more than I thought it did; but what he said to me hurt too. I knew he was going to always hold that over my head, even ten years from now. I just figured that was the type of person that he was.

"Don't worry about it. You don't have to do shit else for me or my kids. Come on Jaquile!"

"Don't you bring your ass out that room!" I narrowed my eyes at him.

"Don't yell at my son."

"You and your son can get the hell out my house." I looked at him in disbelief. Was he really putting me out of his house? I tried to read his face, but nothing was there. He was giving up on me.

"Just let me get my kids and I'll be on my way."

"My daughter isn't going anywhere with you." I made a sarcastic laugh.

"Yeah, okay." I began to walk to the back of the apartment to get my children when Jermaine grabbed my arm and yanked me around. "Get off me Jermaine." I said to trying to yank my arm away but he had a tight grip on me.

"If you wanna go somewhere you better find another way." He extended his hand out. "Give me my car keys." I just looked at him. "I'm serious, give me my keys." I tried to walk away again but he did the same thing again, yanked me back.

"Bitch, give me my fuckin keys!" he yelled in a stern voice. Angel came out the room with Jade in her arms and looked at us. *'I'll show you what a bitch is.'* I thought to myself.

"Alright let go of my arm so I could get them." He let go of my arm and I took the keys out my jacket pocket and slapped him across the face with them leaving a long gash across the face. "I'm a fuckin bitch Jermaine?"

"Ahh fuck!" he screamed. I looked him dead in his eyes and watched him as he hit me dead in the mouth. Angel mouth flew open when she seen him hit me. I took my jacket off and went for it. Jaquile was crying and yelling for me. Angel had Jade in her arms screaming for Jermaine to stop hitting me. I was hitting him like he was somebody out in the streets, and he was hitting my ass back like a nigga. I was screaming all types of *fuck yous* and telling him how much I hated his stupid ass. During the brawl we knocked over lamps and pictures, making a big mess in the living room.

"Jermaine, stop hitting her like that!" I heard Angel yell. Hate is a strong word but I don't think it could explain the feelings that I had for him at that moment. He caught my hand and held a tight grip on me and wouldn't let me go; he took and threw me into the wall, holding me up by my neck.

"Don't do no stupid shit like that anymore." He told me. Blood came down his cheek. With everything in my power I held back the spit that I had in my mouth in which I wanted to throw into his face. He snatched his keys out my hand and let me go.

"Jaquile go in the room and lay down. Ya'll ain't going no got-damn where tonight." Jaquile went in his room, followed by Jermaine and Jade. Angel came towards me with tears in her eyes.

"I'm sorry, I didn't know he could get like this Ne-Ne." tears swelled in my eyes. I didn't want her to see that her brother had defeated me.

"I just want my kids." The tears could be heard as I talked.

"No, just go Ne-Ne. let him cool off and come back tomorrow." I looked at her. My heart was shattering into millions of pieces. I picked my coat up off of the floor and put it on when Jermaine came out of the room. I took one last look at him before I left out of the apartment.

Chapter 14

I caught the bus all the way on the other side of town to Heaven's house. On my way over there I thought about how I fought for his respect. I put up with all his bullshit and tantrums. I thought about how I was always by his side when he was sick, I sat in the hospital for over a week when he had phenomena, but while I had to stay in the hospital for weeks at a time dealing with the kemo-therapy he was nowhere to be found. I felt I deserved better than that. Then there were times I felt I deserved less than what God has given me. My feelings were on an emotional rollercoaster and I didn't know what to do. I wanted to leave Jermaine but my heart belonged to him and there was nothing that I could do. Yes, he did provide for us, he loved me when everyone else used and abused me; but that still doesn't give him the right to sleep with other females whenever he wants. Or use me as a punching bag whenever he gets pissed off at me. I know that I was wrong for hitting him first, but I've been hurt too many damn times. Two wrongs don't make a right. Silent tears continued to fall from my eyes as I walked up to Heavens town home she shared with her husband Thomas. By time I reached the house it was nine o'clock that night.

I knocked on Heavens door with my hat low on my head and a pair of sunglasses on my face, but there wasn't sun out. Heaven opened the door in her oversized t-shirt and a scarf wrapped around her head.

"What's going on?" she asked me allowing me to come into her luxurious home. Her home reminded me of Ms. Harrison's, so cozy and filled with love.

"I need a break from Jermaine for a while," I told her as I sat down on the couch. She sat down beside me.

"Where's the kids?" she asked me. A few tears managed to slip out of my eyes

"Awe, what's wrong?" her face was filled with concern. She wrapped her hand around my shoulder and I flinched. She sat up.

"Take off that hat and sun glasses." I hesitated before I took them off.

"What happened to your face?" she touched my face. I had a bruised cheek, a busted lip and a black eye.

"Um…Jermaine and I were fighting; but I'm alright."

"Fighting, he put his hands on you like that?" I just looked at her. "Were the babies there?" I nodded my head. She took a deep breath then stood up.

"But Angel had them in the room." I tried to cover up. "I just need you to take me to go and get them first thing in the morning." She looked at me. "Please," she nodded her head, and then stretched her hand out.

"Come on," I stood up and followed her in the guest bedroom. She left out of the room and came back with a night gown, "Go get cleaned up," I nodded my head; before I got a chance to leave out of the room she touched my face.

"Are you sure? It doesn't look to good Ne-Ne." I pushed her hand away from my face, tired and annoyed.

"Yes I'm sure." I moved around her and into the bathroom shutting the door behind me. I turned on the shower and began to undress myself. As I was taking off my shirt I had seen bruises on my back. I quickly ripped my shirt off. Tears quickly formed and came out of my eyes. I stepped into the shower and let the warm water fall onto my sore body as I slid down into the tub and cried like I've never cried before.

We parked outside of Jermaine's apartment building until we seen him leave for work the next morning. As soon as I seen his black explorer pulls out of the parking lot I got out and went into the building and up to the apartment door. I banged on the door three times until Angel came and opened the door. I walked past her and into the kids room. She came in behind me.

"Nevaeh what are you doing here?"

"I'm coming to get my kids." I told her then went and picked Jade up. She lifted her head up then placed it back down and went to sleep. I picked up her diaper bag off of her changing table, and then left out of her room and into Jaquile's room. I woke him up and told him to put some pants and some shoes.

"Ne-Ne, Jermaine is going to kill you." I rolled my eyes as I walked back into living room.

"Fuck your brother. Tell him if he wants to see his daughter he can come to my sister house and see her. He knows where she lives." With that said I left out of the house with my kids in my arms. Once I got into the car I turned to my big sister.

"Heaven, can you watch them until I come back?"

"Where are you going?"

"I want to go and visit mommy," I sighed. "I need to get something off of my chest." She smiled at me then nodded her head.

*

"How are you?" I asked her as I sat down. She didn't say anything to me though. "I see your better now. These seven years has been so hard for me. Why didn't you come and look for me? I had to grow up so fast, sleeping with men from time to time just to get what I needed. I got two beautiful kids though." I pulled out a picture of Jermaine, Jade, Jaquile, Angel and I and pointed to each one of us. "This handsome one right here is Jaquile; he's turning six in July. This princess is Jade; she's two months. This is Angel, Jermaine's sister. I don't think she likes me mush but Jermaine tells me not to worry about her. Finally Jermaine, he's the love of my life…Yeah he made this bruise on my face; we were fighting over some stupid shit. But look he asked me to marry him; I told him I had to think about it. Oh, I got into Howard University. I'm majoring in accounting; I'm going too start as soon as the baby turns one." I burst into tears. "You didn't come and find me. I was only ten! A little girl out in the streets on her own! Did you not care about me, about us, Heaven and me? God, I miss you mommy! I wasn't gonna come. I missed you so much-I'm glad Heaven talked me into coming to see you because I wasn't gonna come. I hated you so much for letting them men do what they did to me; I was mad at you for turning me into who I was. But I had to learn to forgive, but I will never forget. I just came by to tell you what's been going on and that I forgive you; and that I also have cancer and I will be going in for surgery soon to get it removed. I also wanted to let you know that I love you and I always will." I felt a cold draft. I wiped my face and stood up, dusting myself off. She didn't say anything tough the whole conversation, I wasn't mad at her. I leaned down kissing the tombstone while placing the flowers on her grave. "I'll be back Thanksgiving, this time with the whole family." I felt another cold draft. "Don't worry daddy, you'll meet Jermaine next time around." I leaned down kissing his tombstone and coming back up with a smile.

Heaven buried her right next to daddy. It felt so good to talk to her. I walked over to the cab that I came in and got in. I began to cry, crying because my mommy wouldn't hurt anymore, crying because she finally had daddy, crying just to cry. Heaven told me she died from an overdose. It hurt me bad, bad to my heart.

Once I left the cemetery I caught the bus and rode to a payphone and called Heaven. She answered on the third ring. I heard Jade crying in the background. I wanted to rush to the house and nurture my baby, but I couldn't. I need to be by myself for awhile, I needed to find myself get on the road into becoming a better person.

"Hello?" Heaven said into the phone. I didn't say anything until she said hello again.

"Heaven?"

"Yes, who's calling?" she asked.

"It's me Nevaeh,"

"Oh, wassup? You want me to some and pick you up?"

"No, but I need a favor." I was on the verge of tears and Heaven could tell.

"What is it baby, why are you about to cry?"

"Can you please take care of my babies for me?" I sniffed. "If Jermaine come for them tell him tell him that I'm sorry, I'm so sorry I just needed to figure some things out. Let him take the kids, but check up on them and ensure that they know that I love them very much." I cried.

"Ne-Ne just come home we can work this out together." She begged me.

"I gotta learn to do things on my own." I told her before I hung up the phone.

*

"Nevaeh get up," I heard someone say as I lay sprawled across the bed. I peeked one of my eyes opened and looked at Key'Shawn. I had been staying with him for a month, just to get my head in the right place. I had nowhere else to turn. I was not staying with Janette because Brandon lived there, and I couldn't stay with heaven because he expected me to be there. I went to Key'Shawn because I knew what we had been over. No matter how much we've flirted since I been there it hasn't gone beyond that. I just couldn't stoop that low to go back to the life that I use to have, as hard as I worked to get where I was. No, it wasn't going to happen.

"What do you want Shawn?" I asked still tired.

"Jermaine is on his way over here, so yeah you have to be up outta here before he comes." He told me. I closed my eyes back. Why no does he want to come and visit? He never came before, this whole moth that I was staying there, now he wants to come. I opened both of my eyes to see Key'Shawn still looking at me.

"What?"

"Come on now, you need to get up and get some clothes on."

"I am up." I told him.

"Nevaeh, ya'll don't live too far from here, so you better stop playing before it's too late." He told me. I sighed then sat up in the bed. I stretched and then got up and went to grab my towel. "You don't have time for that, take it over your sister house." I sucked my teeth and grabbed my pants and threw them on and then threw on my tennis shoes.

"Do I have time to wash my face and brush my teeth?" he nodded his head. I went into the bathroom and washed my face and brushed my teeth. Once I stepped out of the bathroom I went back into the room and grabbed my bags. I looked around the room hoping that I didn't forget anything and left.

I caught the orange line train all the way to New Carrollton Metro station and walked the rest of the way to Heaven's house cold as hell, bundled up in this big leather coat that I took from out of Key'Shawn's closet. I knocked on the door and heard Jaquile's voice. I smiled. I missed my babies and I was finally going to see them after a long and hard month of being away. I knocked three more times before someone came and answered the door. I was pulled into the house while being embraced in my sister arms.

"Hey!" I said embracing her back.

"I missed you!" she looked behind me at my bags. "You're staying?" I smiled. She smiled back.

"Where's my kids?" I asked her.

"In the living room playing." I came out of my coat as I walked into the living room. I threw the coat on the arm of the chair and watched as Jaquile played with his action figures as he watched transformers.

"Hey baby," I said. He turned around and once he realized it was me his eyes lit up.

"Mommy!" he shrieked. I smiled and welcomed him with open arms as he jumped into my, grabbing me around my neck for dear life. Afraid that I might leave him, yet again; but I wasn't going to leave my kids anymore.

"Mommy missed you." I told him as tears squeezed out of my eyes.

"I missed you too. Were you mad at me? Is that why you keep

leaving?" he questioned. He had the saddest look on his face that I had ever seen.

"No baby, you can never make me that mad to the point that I want to leave you. Mommy just needed a break for awhile." I assured him. I kissed his forehead. "Go ahead and play while I talk to your auntie." Without hesitation he went back over to his spot in front of the T.V. and got back into the program he was watching. I stood up and followed Heaven into the kitchen. I sat at one of the bar stools while she poured us something to drink.

"It feels so good to be back home." I said as I inhaled deeply.

"Where were you staying?" she questioned.

"With Key'Shawn," her head quickly looked my way. She narrowed her eyes.

"Key'Shawn, as in the Key'Shawn you use to have sex with?" I nodded my head as I quickly spoke.

"But we didn't do anything. I just stayed with him because he was the last place that Jay would've expected me to be." I told her.

"Uh huh," was all she said.

"You know while I was there I did a lot of thinking. Maybe Jay and I are right for each other. I think I am ready to settle down with him; it's time for us to be a family. Jaquile needs a male role model in his life and Jade definitely needs a father there. I don't want her to go through the same shit as I did." I said. She came and sat on the stool next to me.

"When are you doing home?" I asked her.

"Tonight."

I walked into the apartment scared as hell. My hands were shaking and I had butterflies in my stomach. The place still looked the same, he didn't change anything. I looked around to see if anyone was in the kitchen and bathroom. No one; but I heard music coming from out of one of the rooms. The place was clean, nothing out of place. Just like Jermaine, he never did like a dirty house. I walked to our room, that's where the music was coming from, and opened the door. The soothing sound of Maxwell voice echoed through the room as he sung *'A Woman's Work.'* I looked at Jermaine as he slept peacefully. I turned to walk out of the room, when I heard him speak.

"Are you back to stay, or are you coming to get more of your things?" he asked. I turned and looked at him. He was now standing out of the bed, he was still fully dressed.

"If it's okay with you, I would like to come back home." I looked down at my feet as I spoke.

"Why should I let you come back? Do you honestly think that you deserve to come back into this house after up and leaving like you did?" I just stared at him. I began to breathe heavily trying not to cry.

"Yes I do. Is it wrong for me to try and get myself together? I told my sister where I was at so she shouldn't have to worry. At the time that I left I gave a damn about you, if you want me to be honest." I told him. He began to walk up closer to me as he nodded his head. I got nervous. I didn't want to have a repeat of what had happened before I left. I closed my eyes afraid that he was going to go up aside my head when he took me in his arms and hugged me, swaying me back and forth. He kissed my forehead.

"Don't you ever in your life disappear like that again. Got me all scared and shit." I chuckled. *Good, that's what his ass gets for hitting me like that.* I looked up at him and smiled.

"I wrote a poem while I was gone." I told him.

"Oh yeah, you writing again?" he asked as he looked down into my eyes. I nodded my head.

"You wanna hear it?" I questioned.

"Yeah let me see what you got." I cleared my throat like I was about to sing some high pitch song. He laughed, as did I. I recited the poem to him like I've never done before.

"Make love to me Jermaine."

"Huh?" Jermaine asked.

"Make me feel good. Make me cum over and over again." Jermaine moved me over to the bed and climbed on top of me while kissing me. I slowly relaxed in his arms as his hands soothingly traced every curve of my body. Gently planting butterfly kisses from my neck to my navel. I felt as his hands firmly grasped my hips and he took my clit into his mouth; rolling his tongue in and out of me, making me moan his name in so much pleasure, like I was on ecstasy. My hands gripping to the sheets like I was holding on for dear life, he held my hips tighter with his tongue going deeper, making circles inside of me. I arched my back as my eyes rolled to the back of my head and screamed when I came. I let my body relax and open my eyes to focus my attention back to him.

I watched as he climbed back on the bed and slowly pushed my legs apart and climbed between them. He positioned himself on top of me and began to lick my ear while my hands found their way to his long, hard dick. I could hear him groaning in my ear as I stroked it up and down with long, slow strokes. When I pulled my hand away I immediately felt pain as he entered me. I let out small, mixed with pain and pleasure until I heard him say, "I got you babe," as he slowly pushed his self inside of me. Not knowing how he did it, I just held onto him, digging my nails into his back until the pain ceased. He has a lot of scratch marks on his back, that's starting to fade away, because somehow he always manages to make it feel like the first time every time. I felt him as he grinded inside of me, the pain had gone and pleasure and ecstasy had completely taken over my body. An hour into our love making I felt the liquids our bodies created had made, in between us, making him slide in and out of me with much ease. I held on tight to him as I came, like always he took care of my needs first then his. A couple minutes later I looked up and watched his face as he exploded.

Chapter 16

It was a month before Janette's wedding and things were crazy. We were trying to make sure everyone gowns were fitting; she was putting last minute touches on her wedding dress. I was sitting in the bathroom washing Jade, getting ready for us to go out and have a girls day out with Janette and Heaven, when my phone rang.

"Answer my phone Jaquile," I yelled. Moments later he came in handing me my phone. "Hello?" I said into the phone.

"Watch your motha-fuckin back bitch," TaNeesha said on the other end.

"How the fuck you get my cell phone number?" I questioned her.

"Don't worry about that, you just watch your back."

"You talking all that shit, bring your ass over here and do something. Do you need the address?" I said as the anger over whelmed my body.

"Aight, and no I don't need the damn address. I know it all too well from the numerous nights that I spent over there. I'll be there!" with that said she hung up the phone.

I finished washing Jade and laid her down to sleep, soon after someone had knocked on my door. I went and opened the door without looking through the peep hole. I opened the front door then suddenly felt a strong pain in my face. When I came to I saw a girl with golden brown hair and a red skin tone. I figured she was Taneesha so I just wiled out on her. I'm not even going to lie, she put up a good fight, until Jermaine walked into the house. He pulled us apart and that's when I kicked her in the stomach.

"I thought you told that *BITCH* to stop callin here!" I shouted at Jermaine.

Standing in between the both of us he said, "I did. Why is she here?"

"To get you back," TaNeesha said while moving closer to him. He pushed her back.

"Why? I don't want you," Jermaine told her. TaNeesha's facial expression changed from flirtatious to angry, to obsessed. "What, what you mean you don't want me?"

"Like he said bitch, he doesn't want your ass. Get that through your thick ass skull and get the fuck up out my house." I told her.

"Nevaeh chill, damn. Tish, I can't be with you. I am engaged I can't mess with you anymore." Jermaine told her.

"Aight I respect that. Can I get a hug before I leave?" she asked. Jermaine looked at me and I gave him this stern look as if to say no.

"Naw,"

"Can you at least walk me to my car?" she asked desperately.

"Yeah, come on."

"Jermaine?" He turned around and kissed me, assuring me that he wasn't going anywhere. I watched them walk out of the house. He said that it was over with them, and I believe him, but it's that girl. She was just too damn sneaky for my blood. *'At least she wasn't ugly,'*

I sat on the couch waiting for him to come back in the house. He was gone just a little too long, but then I heard someone running up the stairs, I thought it was him but it wasn't. Someone began to bang on my door like they were the damn police. I swung the door open.

"Damn Nicole, you banging on the door like the damn police." My neighbor's chest rapidly moved in and out as she tried to speak.

"Jay, Jay," she swallowed hard. "Jay just got shot." All I could think was not again. I couldn't lose someone I loved by a bullet, yet again. I rushed out of the house with Nicole right behind me. There was a crowd formed around him by the time I made it outside. I pushed through them and seen him on the ground blood was all around him. I fell down beside him and prayed to God like my life depended on it.

*

I sat down hospital bed holding his hand and rocking Jade to sleep while Jaquile sat on the couch watching the television. I looked down at Jade sleeping peacefully in my arms.

"Baby," Jermaine called. I looked at him and smiled.

"Hey baby,"

"That dumb bitch shot me." Jermaine said.

"You scared me, I thought you were gonna die on me." I told him.

"Awe, I'm sorry. Give me a kiss," I leaned over and gave him a peck on the lips.

"Awe that little kiss. Give me another one." I smiled and gave him another one. He parted my lips with his tongue and invited me into a passionate kiss.

"Uh hmmm," I heard someone clear his or her throat. I broke the kiss then turned around. I had seen Heaven standing by the door with Janette and Brandon behind her. Sitting back down in the chair I spoke.

"Hey ya'll,"

"Wassup," Janette and Brandon said in unison. Heaven walked over to Jermaine and gave him a small hug.

"Hey brotha-in-law, how you feelin?" Heaven asked.

"Oh, I'm good now you know just a lil tired." Jermaine told her. She nodded her head.

"Yeah, you need to be getting your rest" Heaven said.

"Yup, so where my man at?" Jermaine asked Heaven.

"He at work," my sister said as she sat down.

"That niggas always at work," I told her.

"Well, we gotta pay the bills." She said. I just nodded my head and handed Jade to her.

"Yeah, hold her for me, I gotta go to the bathroom." I stood up.

"I gotta go too; Nevaeh can you show me where it is?" unsure I said yeah. Brandon and I walked out the room and down the hall.

"Alright, the men's bathroom is right there," I pointed across the hall. "I'll meet you back in the room," I told Brandon.

"Aight, but come here," he said.

"What?" I asked him.

"Just come here," reluctantly I went to him. He pulled me into a kiss. I pushed him back away from me.

"What are you doing?" I asked disgusted and confused.

"Why you push me away like you ain't wanna kiss me?"

"Cause I didn't."

"You say something when I kiss you, but when I was all up in your shit you ain't say nothing," When those words left his mouth my fist connected with his face.

"Don't you ever come near me again; if you do I will *kill* you," I said sternly. After that I didn't have to go to the bathroom anymore, I walked back to the room to find Jermaine, Heaven, and Janet talking and the kids asleep. Minutes after I walked in Brandon came in with a bruise and a lump growing on his face. Janette turned around and looked at us as I started to make my way to the bed.

"Baby what happened to your face?" Janette asked him. Pointing to me Brandon said,

"That bitch hit me. I should have smacked her ass back."

"Dog why the fuck you callin my girl a bitch man. Don't you ever disrespect her again, do it again and your ass is gonna be the one lying in this bed. I don't give a fuck what she did to you." Jermaine told him. Janette rolled her eyes at Jermaine then looked back at Brandon.

"Why did she hit you?" Brandon looked at me then back at janette before saying,

"Nevaeh kissed me, I pushed her ass away. She got mad cause I told her that I didn't want her, so she hit me." When he said that it felt like all the breath had left my body, I started to breathe heavily as everyone just stared at me. Tears started to roll down my cheeks as I screamed.

"Why the fuck you lyin on me. All that shit you and your boys did to me in the car," I turned to Jermaine, Janette, and Heaven and continued to talk. "him and two other boys raped me while Key'Shawn watched; why don't you tell them that shit!" Janette looked at Brandon in disbelief, "Is that true?"

"Hell naw I didn't rape that girl. I'm not gonna lie, I did have sex with her but she was willing to do it." He answered with convincing eyes. Hell I even believed him if you looked at the type of background I had. Janette walked over to Jermaine and laid Jade in his arms. She then stood by Brandon.

"So this is how you do best friends Ne-Ne? I always knew you were a damn hoe. I knew you wanted him." Tears began to pour out of my eyes. It hurts for someone you loved so much, who ment more to you than any nigga in this world to think so less of you.

"You gonna believe this nigga over me? You know that I would never fuck with a nigga that you been with,"

"Yeah, that's the same shit I thought; but I know you, and I know how you roll." I looked back at my sister and fiancé only for them to be staring back at me. "I knew all that shit they were saying about you in school was true, but I didn't want to believe it. As far as I'm concerned this fucking friendship is over. Come on Brandon." Brandon turned around with a smirk on his face as he followed Janette out the door. I tried to call after her so I could tell her the truth but she just ignored me. I turned and looked at the only two people I have left in this world.

"Why did you let her carry you like that?" was the first thing out of

Heaven's mouth.

"What the fuck was I suppose to do Heaven?"

"Something, you just let her sit up there and carry you like you ain't shit."

"Because I-" Jermaine cut me off.

"No, that's enough, stop with this shit." Jermaine said. I looked at him. "Heaven, take the kids to get something to eat, please." Heaven grabbed Jade out of Jermaine arms then woke Jaquile up, moments later they left out of the room. I stood at the foot of Jermaine's bed.

"Come here," he said. I took a seat in the chair beside the bed. "Are you okay?"

"I just lost my best friend; I'm just so tired of people gangin up on me. Heaven suppose to be my damn sister, I should've left her ass in the damn hospital."

"No, baby you love your sister. She just wants the best for you. As far as Janette is concerned, she'll come around. She's just blinded by that nigga." I just shook my head.

"So, he was one of the niggas who raped you?" Jermaine asked. I just nodded my head yes. "He lucky I'm in this damn hospital right now, when I get out I'ma beat his ass."

"Don't worry about it Jay," I told him.

"Naw man, I'm tired of you leaving shit alone and letting those niggas hurt you," Jermaine said. I just left it alone because he was just going to go on and on about it.

The police caught TaNeesha a couple days later and charged her with attempted murder and assault with a deadly weapon. When Jermaine got out the hospital he did exactly what he said he was going to do. He went to Janette's house and beat the shit out of Brandon. He whopped his ass until he confessed the whole thing to Janette. She called off the wedding. For a whole two weeks she called me, wanting to apologize I guess. Maybe one day we would be friends again, but not that day.

Chapter 17

We decided to have our wedding that following year. I choose Heaven to be my maid of honor and two other girls that I met back in high school to be my brides maids. I incited Janette to be at the wedding but she was not going to be in it, not after she called me all of that.

I was sitting in the kitchen fixing the kids something to eat while they watched television. Jade was now one and Jaquile was six, looking just like me. Anyway I was fixing them something to eat when I heard the front door open then close and Heaven appeared in the kitchen doorway.

"Wassup Ne-Ne?" Heaven asked.

"Nothing, what you doin here?" I questioned her.

"Oh, I got a surprise for you," she answered.

"What is it?" I asked as I moved from the fridge to the stove.

"Look," I looked towards Heaven and seen a woman with golden brown skin and long, thin, full sandy brown hair with streaks of red and just a hint of grey peeking through. I knew I seen her before, she looked to be in her early forties. She looked at me and smiled waiting for me to say something.

"Oh, so now you don't remember me," the woman said. I stared at the lady as I lifted one of my eye brows. "Aight, let me see if you remember this," she grabbed her stomach and kneeled down to the floor. I don't feel good. I want my mommy." The lady said. She giggled as she stood to her feet. I laughed as I went in and gave her a hug.

"Ms. Harrison how are you?" I asked.

"Good girl and its Mrs. Proctor now." I smiled. She had finally gotten married."So I hear you're getting married."

"Yes, oh my goodness you're here, I've been thinking about you for so long," I said freaking out. I pulled back from the hug. "Come meet the kids," I said dragging her into the living room where the kids were. I picked Jade up and handed her to Ms. Harrison.

"This is Jade," she took Jade in her arms and smiled. "Come here Jaquile baby," I called. He came walking over with his face still in the television. "And this big boy is my baby," I kissed him on his forehead as he leaned into my arms. "What do you say Jaquile?"

"Hi," he said still into the television. We laughed at him. We sat and talked for hours about everything that has happened with us. I managed to leave out my promiscuous ways.

"Sweetie I have something to tell you," Ms. Harrison told me.

"Okay," I retorted with a smile on my face.

"I think I should talk to you in private,"

My smile slowly left my face, "Naw I'm cool right here. Tell me what you gotta say."

"Okay," Ms. Harrison sighed then looked at Heaven. I watched as Heaven closed her eyes and nodded her head. My eyes shifted back and forth to the both of them.

"What? Why do ya'll keep looking at each other like that? What's going on?"

"I'm your birth mother," Ms. Harrison blurted out. I just looked at her trying to absorb what she had just told me.

"What?" I asked shocked.

"I'm your birth mother," I got up off the couch then said,

"Excuse me," I walked past Heaven and into my room. I had my head in my hands sobbing when Heaven came in there and sat beside me on the bed. I looked up at her with red eyes.

"I don't get it, so you not really my sister?" I asked Heaven. She looked at me,

"Yeah I'm your sister but mommy just isn't your mommy," I embraced her into a hug and cried.

"Why she didn't want me?" hugging me she said,

"Why don't you ask your mother?" I lifted up my head and looked at her; she gave me a hug then got up and left out the room. I was sitting in my vanity fixing my face when Ms. Harrison, my mother, came in. I looked at her through the mirror as she shut the bedroom and made her way over to the bed and sat down

"Did you not want me or something? Was I a mistake? Was I too much to handle? Come on tell me something!" I semi yelled with an attitude.

"No Nevaeh, sweetheart listen. It wasn't the fact that I didn't want you, I was young, and I wasn't ready for a child." Ms. Harrison tried to explain.

"How old were you?" I asked her.

"Sixteen," she answered.

"I was thirteen when I had my first child and I wasn't ready, and last August I had Jade and I still wasn't ready but I had to do what I had to do. So what makes you think that you're ready now?" Tears began to roll out of my eyes.

"I been ready since that time you lost your first tooth. I was ready as soon as I turned eighteen.

"So why didn't you come and get me?"

"Because of your father," I turned and looked at her.

"Who is my father?" Ms. Harrison sighed.

"Your father is Jonathon; but the one you been calling mommy is really your aunt, my sister."

"Well what does my dad have to do with you taking custody? He died when I was three."

"I didn't have any rights, and your aunt, my sister, adopted you, so she had become your legal guardian.

We talked and talked about how her and my father got together, and about her wanting to be in my life. My father cheated on my mom with Ms. Harrison and ended up pregnant with me at sixteen and my dad was twenty-one. What did he want with a sixteen-year old? I don't know. She said that they were going at it for a while, when my mom found out she was pissed; kicked her out pregnant and all. To be honest I would have done the same thing, but I would've kicked the man out as well. See she lived with my mom because their mom died when Ms. Harrison turned fifteen and neither one of their fathers stuck around. We talked some more until Jermaine came home. I introduced him and Ms. Harrison to each other as they shook hands. I introduced her as my mother, she looked at me and smiled and Jermaine looked at me confused.

"I'll tell you about it later," I told Jermaine. He nodded his head then walked back out of the room.

After Ms. Harrison left, around nine o'clock that night, I couldn't stop thinking about her. It was hard to believe it but deep down I always wanted her as my mother. In some way I was happy but in another way I wasn't, I wasn't about to rush into calling her mommy because I still had respect for the woman who cared for me for them eight in a half years. Even though she abused alcohol and drugs, she still gave me a roof over top of my head, food in my stomach and put clothes on my back. Our home wasn't a happy home but I had to make due until she let them men take advantage of me. Then again I still love her, Ms. Harrison might have been my birth mother but Mrs. Lawanda White will always be the mother I call mommy.

Prison Without Bars

Be careful of what you wish for.

Travel through the life of April, a twenty year old college student. April struggles to raise her one-year old daughter while trying to figure out her sexuality.

Still sleeping with her baby father, Bryan, she becomes pregnant again sending her into post-pardon depression. Coping with her depression April starts hanging with Misharo, a girl who was known to get people hooked on drugs. April thought drugs was the worst of her problems until she met Aiden.

Aiden, a junkie that April had met in a crack house, used and abused April to the best of his ability. There was not a day that had went by that he wasn't pulling the strings, making her do what he wanted.

Will April ever be able to be set free from his captivity?

Turn the page for a preview

Chapter One

"Common law is an old English law which is created from everyday social customs, rules, and practices. The common law has a big impact on the American criminal justice system." I studied out loud to myself. Mid terms was five hours away and I wasn't ready. If only Bryan would've picked Kaylah up like he said he was going to do I could've been had my head in my books. Last minute cramming is what I call it. I tried to reposition myself in the process one of my text books fell on the floor causing a loud noise. I shut my eyes tight hoping that I didn't wake Kaylah. I turned my head just in time to see her little head pop up. She looked at me then began to whimper once she seen that I wasn't coming over to sooth her. She let out a loud cry.

"Damn," I mumbled. "Shh, what's wrong with mommy's baby?" I said as I walked over to my one year old daughter and picked her up. As soon as I picked her up she quiet down as if she was never crying. "You just spoiled you know that?" I told her. She smiled at me like she understood what I was saying. I smiled as well.

Knock, knock

"April, you still up?"

"Yes ma'am, you can come in." I was walking around my room trying to rock Kaylah back to sleep when my mother came in.

"Why aren't you asleep?" she asked as she grabbed the baby out of my arms. I moved from the middle of my floor back down to my study area which consisted of a bean bag pillow and a dim light in the corner.

"Because, I have mid-terms tomorrow and I

haven't studied all day. Bryan promised me that he was going to come and get Kay-Kay, but he never came." My mother rolled her eyes and shook her head before she spoke. "Aight, I'm gonna take my grandbaby and put her back to sleep when I come back in an hour I should see you finishing up. I don't want you falling asleep on the test instead of taking it."

"Yes ma'am." She smiled at me then headed out of the room with my daughter still in her arms.

***

"April! April!"

'What does this girl want?' I thought to myself. I put on a tired smile as I turned around. "Hey, wassup Raegan?" she threw her arm around my waist.

"Nothing," she said. "What happened to you this past week?"

"What are you talking about?"

"I been tryna call your ass all week. I was tryna get sometime in to chill with you but you been ignoring my calls." We were walking down the quad and to the front of the campus.

"Oh nah it's nothing like that; but I do have a child and I had to study for mid-terms." I seen her nod her head out the corner of my eye. I watched as she looked at me with pure lust in her eyes.

"I thought Bryan was picking her up."

"I thought so as well, but he never came." She shook her head.

"Um, see that's why I don't like niggas," she said. I smirked. "So you comin over my house when you get off of work?" I shook my head.

"Well damn, what's wrong with you?"

"I'm just not really in the mood to be bothered with today." We stopped stood in front of each other. Her hands rested on my waist, I became uncomfortable as she pulled me closer. I tried to back away from her but her grip wouldn't let me.

"Stop playing April, I'm not going to bite your ass." She knew I didn't like public intimacy.

"Raegan you know I don't do the public shit."

"No, you just not comfortable with your sexuality yet; when you and Bryan were together ya'll were basically fucking in public; so don't give me that." I sighed. She was right I was still trying to get use to the whole lesbian thing. I was trying to adjust to the stares as we held hands and kissed in public. I looked at her starring at me.

"What?" I questioned.

"I missed your sexy ass." I blushed. I took a step back and looked over her breath taking body biting my lip. She smiled.

She was a mix breed; red bone chick. She possessed an hour glass shape. Her b-cup breast were always perky, just like I liked them, she didn't have much ass but that was okay with me just as long as it was enough there for me to grip while I was eating her insides out. She had small pink lips and a beauty mark on the left side of her mouth. If you didn't know, you would've thought she was Hispanic just by her complexion and her hair texture; which she kept down to her shoulders.

"How you getting to work?" Raegan asked me.

"Bryan supposed to come and get me." Raegan scrunched her face up.

"What?" I asked her.

"I aint know that nigga was picking you up." I gave her this look as if to say 'Bitch stop lying.' She frowned up at my face.

"I don't like him. He keeps starring up at me like

he wants to get in my panties." I laughed at her.

"He doesn't like your ass either," she sucked her teeth.

"Why, cause I took his girl from him." I chuckled.

"Whatever," she laughed then pulled me closer to her.

"Ha, I turned that pussy out baby?" she pecked my lips.

I smiled.

She kissed me again.

My panties moistened.

"April!" I stepped back away from Raegan and looked to see who was calling me. It was Bryan. I put a finger up letting him know that I would be just a minute. I looked back at Raegan.

"Make his ass wait," she said giving Bryan the evil eye. I laughed.

"I gotta go before I be late for work." She smacked her lips.

"Aight, but you gonna call me when you get off of work right."

"Of course." I told her.

"Okay, give me another kiss before you leave." Just as I was about to give her a peck on her lips Bryan called me again.

"April if you don't bring yo' ass on." I laughed, quickly gave my girl a kiss, and then walked over to Bryan.

"That shit is just nasty," Bryan expressed as we pulled out of the campus parking lot. "My daughter is not gonna be a dyke." I smacked my lips and then looked out the window.

"She can be whatever she wanna be."

"Yeah whateva pooh," he said calling me by the nickname he gave me when we first met. I thought it was cute but I never understood why he called me that. He placed his hand on my thigh. I pushed it away.

"Don't touch me," he gave a little chuckle.

"That's how it is now?"

"That's how it's been. You gonna call people trifflin when you're the one that's trifflin."

"Oh lawd, what you talking about?"

"What happened to you this week?"

"I had to work," he said.

"Whateva happened to you calling and telling me that you wouldn't be able to pick her up. You know I had mid-terms,"

"Well what do you want me to do now? It's over. Stop with all that dwelling on the past."

"I can't stand your dumb ass." He smiled, and then placed his hand back on my thigh and began to massage it; inching his way to my coochie.

"I swear I hate your ass. Stop touchin me Bryan,"

"You hate me Pooh?" I couldn't help but to suppress a tiny smile. His hand massaged my clit.

"Yeah I hate you," I opened my legs wider and closed my eyes because it felt too damn good.

He stopped.

He laughed. He moved his hand away. He knew what he was doing.

"Fake ass dyke," he laughed some more. I smacked my lips and then looked back out the window. I sighed. "I'm just sayin what real lesbian still fucks her baby fatha?" he asked.

"Shut up," I folded my arms over my tiny breast.

"Like be honest with me now, because I honestly and truly would like to know."

"What Bryan?"

"Why the hell you start liking females?"

"I donno, I've always been attracted to them," I told him.

"So you like the taste of that twat?" he laughed as he plucked my lips. I smacked his hand away.

"Shut up and drive." I told him. He was truly irritating me at that point. There were days when we got along and then there would be the days where I couldn't stand his ass, and those days started rolling around more frequently. I guess that's why we didn't work out.

Made in the USA
Charleston, SC
11 December 2012